WALL
TO
WALL

WALL

TO

WALL

BY
DOUGLAS WOOLF

THE DALKEY ARCHIVE PRESS

LIBRARY OF CONGRESS CATALOGING IN PUBLICATION DATA

Woolf, Douglas.
  Wall to wall.
  I. Title
ISBN 0-916583-06-6
ISBN 0-916583-07-4

THE DALKEY ARCHIVE PRESS
1817 79th Avenue
Elmwood Park, IL 60635

To my first friend

One

Although he smiled, and stepped readily enough aside for the busy walkers, Claude Squires did not enjoy this stroll to work nearly so much as they no doubt thought he did. Just a week ago he had moved six blocks away from the grounds, after one howling night in there, and now he left the room every—every—morning at five to eight, ten minutes late, having made himself that regular. Always he managed to kill a few minutes on the way, stopping here and there to observe some bush, a lawn, some dog or cat. He sensed that to the passers-by and those others who watched him from their windows his passage was unobjectionable at least, while to the old ladies and the girls his leisurely appearance must have been rather appealing, nice. He wore no uniform, only a standard white shirt, grey washable trousers, gayish socks, but hard-toed shoes, in case. All this at some cost to himself, for a white uniform and a small white room on the grounds counted as part of his salary and the controller's office had refused to negotiate; but he considered his anonymity and this space, this filter of sunlight and bougainvillaea he passed through, worth more than they would give out in a fiscal year, should he somehow last that long.

Yet he could not enjoy the walk. In the morning especially a bougainvillaea looks handmade, lawns are always lawns, and it is true indeed that dogs smell fear. Cats don't say. While three blocks along, at the midway mark, his newsboy swayed on the corner crooning the usual "Oh acidophilus toddymake." A thick-trunked ponderosa of a man, he had sparse needled hair and one evasive eye that seemed always ready to slide from its makeshift nest. Claude never bought from him, and his newsboy did not seem to expect him to but held his soiled paper high, high beyond reach, two or three others clamped in the yellowing pit of his nether arm. Whatever stock he had he must have carried inside his shirt or pants, for there was never the tidy, weighted pile nearby. Perhaps he had no need of spares, for he allowed would-be customers to pass him up easily, crooning after them with what seemed relief, as though he could not, could not bear the sight of them. However, everything was changed today. Today he gave off crooning, at the instant Claude came abreast: "And a goodmorning to you too, *sir*," he hissed as plainly as any man ever would. Claude, who always hurried here, was paces past by the time he knew what he had heard, and stopped. What was that for? Turning to look at the swaying back, he reapproached part way. "Sir, it's not you I pass up every morning," he thought he'd like to say. "You're a willing worker, conscientious, that's easily seen. It's that wicked paper you're waving there." But now the windblown nest tipped backward and the eye slid toward him dangerously, beseeching him to remove himself. Shrugging shamefaced Claude hurried on, acidophilus toddymake burning both his ears. He did not stop again and arrived at the gate feeling, more than ever, terrible. "Good day to you, sir," he said.

"How are you today, young man?"

What to say? "Late."

"Well, Yo Carro is running in the eighth."

"He is?"

"Smith is up."

"Ah, he'll win."

"Damn right she will."

At this hour the password was lethargy. Part of the terror was that it did seem almost peaceful here, more peaceful than anywhere else, than anywhere. Nobody ran upon the grounds, even the robins and wrens seemed almost sedate. Along the drives the bread, the meat, the milk, the laundry trucks glided noiselessly by like peddled things. Shiny sprinklers flung hard water everywhere without a sound, each drop being caught by a soft blade of grass. One wondered how all those lawns got mowed; by sheep no doubt. Even the south wing was still, they had had their pills or baths who needed them. Now a little girl laughed, and rounding the women's wing he looked for her despite himself. She stood at the centermost bench amid her big-legged friends in their kimonos and slips, leaning on them. Now she laughed again, for she had caught sight of Claude. When she asked a question of the women they nodded their approval, smiled. One put a final touch on her coiffure. He stood waiting while she shook the morning in her run to him. "Hi, Ann . . . "

"Hi, Claude!"

"What have you there?"

She kept her hands behind her back. "You guess," she said.

"Candy?"

She shook her head.

"Bubblegum?"

"No."

"Acidophilus toddymake?"

Wrong again. She showed him so. It was her hands she held, starfished out, displaying exquisite nails of shiny pink. They had painstakingly pressed her cuticles back, until a glimpse of white shone in the arch of each. Stooping, "What are those?" he asked.

"My moons," she said.

"Ah. I thought."

"Are they pretty?"

Looking he shook his head. "No. Beautiful."

She tipped her hands up for herself to see. "Tomorrow we're going to do my toes."

"Oho."

"Well, goodbye," she said, and he waved as she fled to the bench again. One of the women there waved back at him; her delighted friends slapped at her outflung leg, but smiling she left it so, adjusted her lapels instead. "Hello, Mr. Claude." she called.

He threw a kiss to her.

"Oow," they said. They were flattering him.

Around the south wing and over the half-hearted croquet court, he entered the men's domain, strolled to a table and sat down at it. He was working now. One or two nodded his way, and he smiled back. Crossing his legs he felt his new shirt for the cigarettes. This seemed a little abrupt to him, but he had already committed himself; he tore open the pack too vigorously, because they had seen him hesitate. They accepted his cigarettes in silence, waiting to thank him as he fired them up, those who were not saving theirs. Claude fired himself up last. Tucking the pack away, he felt that he was smoking too much. Now all sat relaxed, a peaceful cloud uniting them. Across the grass the Bailey brothers sat back-to-back under another tree, the younger and slimmer breathing privately on a harmonica. From here their T-shirts looked very clean against their long arms and necks, far out on the grass their big white sneakers stuck up like new, and their dark round heads appeared not so much small as superbly compact things. But Claude alone was looking at them. Beside him Mr. Harris folded his morning newspaper and held it out to Claude. "Seen this yet?"

"No."

"Don't read it," Mr. Harris said, folding the paper once more and sliding it under his rear. "It will only upset you, son."

"It's a wicked paper . . ." Claude agreed, but Mr. Harris was overspeaking him.

"It's the big black words that do it. The little grey ones don't matter very much, they're just fill-ins they take everyday from the wires. They concentrate their poison in the big black words, where it will radiate. Of course if you read the little stories too you've got sure proof that every word they wrote above, themselves, was a fat black lie, but by then you've absorbed a thousand greyer ones, and where and how to check on those? This way the mind deteriorates. The best way you can save yourself is not to read it, son."

"No, I . . ."

"That's right, if you're not careful," Mr. Harris went on, blue-eyed, red-faced, "you find yourself pretty soon hating everyone but God, the Babe, and a few dead senators. That's no fun. Men aren't so bad as that."

"No."

"That's right, you begin to worry about anyone who opens his mouth except to say ho it looks like rain, let's bowl. Otherwise you wonder what the hell he's trying to prove, or undermine. If he asks what time it is, you wonder what terrible thing is scheduled to happen, where it will happen, when. You can't even stand to be asked how you feel today—he's probably looking at the bumps on you, they may have grown more noticeable overnight. Soon you feel you should apologize for standing there where he can watch you dying in front of him, he'd rather for you to carry your head around in a little plaid bag, like your bowling ball. There's no joy in that. Men aren't so very bad." Mr. Harris paused to remove his Panama hat. Water seeped from his knobby forehead, which he mopped with a damp handkerchief. "I've offended you, son," he said.

"Not at all, I entirely agree with you."

Mr. Harris replaced his hat, folded his handkerchief. "I shouldn't shoot off this way," he said. "I read too much."

"No, no. You're right . . ."

Now Claude, waiting for Mr. Harris to add, watched

the younger Bailey brother stand up, languidly unfold himself. Bowing his head a little bit, treading the grass with his big white shoes, he stepped a soft circle around his brother, and around the tree. He circled again. Now you could hear the sweet music in his breathing hands, or imagine so. From just outside the shade of the tree a small old man observed the dance, and he appeared to speak to the Bailey boys. When they paid him little attention he glanced toward the smokers' tree, and quickly aside. But now hitching his pants, eyes downcast, he did begin to make his way toward them, so slowly that no one might ever have known were it not for the dark track his flat bare feet scuffed in the grass. Claude imagined he watched alone, until he found an arm pressed against his chest. It was crooked at the elbow, taut, so that the tendons showed. Claude drew in from it, and from a pale blue warning flash. Underbreath Mr. Harris's voice was pleading though, "Don't try to stop me, son." He waited until the little man had entered their shade, and then he moved with unexpected speed and grace, shoulders hunched and forward, elbows jutting out. The man already was whimpering; he began to wail as Mr. Harris approached. Mr. Harris did not waste time. He grasped the loose trousers in both of his hands as though to tidy them up, and when he turned away the now moaning man stood hobbled there, his hands fluttering around the pitiful brown bit he had to hide. Mr. Harris picked up his newspaper before he sat down, and Claude backed off. "Thank you, son," Mr. Harris seated said, not looking up at Claude. "I wouldn't like to have had to hurt you."

"I didn't know what you were going to do!"

Mr. Harris looked up at him in plain surprise, yet not unkindly, and now with his newspaper gave Claude's arm an encouraging pat. "Well, you're young," he said.

Claude went over to the whimpering man, who had made no effort to retrieve his pants but stood shuffling them, showing how bad things were. Claude, drawing them up, saw that their cord had broken and it couldn't afford a knot. After a moment's fuss, he took off his new leather belt and fixed it around the man, through what loops he had; the belt needed a further hole, but Claude did not carry a knife—he tied it tight. So far he was working without pay today. He patted the old man's shoulder, and now the man looked down at himself and stopped whimpering. Behind them a few men had come over to see. "That looks nice," one said. Patting the thin shoulder again, Claude walked away. His pants stayed up, although he didn't fill them as he had a week ago.

Ahead the Bailey brothers loped over the grass, clearly interrupting him. They stopped and waited a few yards off, a careless geometry of arms and legs. Their smiles seemed lavish in their frugal heads. Claude said good-morning to them.

"We have to go now, boss," the older said.

"Go?"

"We go every Thursday, boss," the younger Bailey explained. Still smiling at Claude he slipped his harmonica into a pocket, bent quickly at the knees to stroke sweet music from a baby grand. "We take lessons, boss."

"Oh, I see." Claude looked questioningly over the piano at Franklin Storrs, just now approaching from the dining hall. Franklin nodded, and Claude nodded in turn to the Bailey brothers. "O.K., boys."

Without a word they turned and trotted, elbow to elbow, loosely in step, across the grounds. Claude and Franklin watched them go.

"Actually you should have told them to leave through the gate, Claude," Franklin said, "so the keeper will know that they've gone. But that's all right. They're O.K. They'll be back in time."

"Why are they here? What's wrong with them?"

"Oh, there's nothing *wrong* there," Franklin said,

looking after the boys. "It's just that when they're drinking they tend to forget what they are. Poor devils, they should be drunk all the time." Removing his heavy-rimmed glasses, he folded them one-handed and with the same deft motion dropped them into his breast pocket. Now he took Claude's arm with the hearty, belittling grip that doctors had when they were leading him toward the door, but Franklin wasn't trying to get rid of Claude: "Claude, there's someone else I want you to meet," he said. "Bronson Leland Stowe, 29, unmarried, two and a half years in med, specialized in gynecology. He was at school with me, although I didn't know him then. (He was a year ahead of me.) A truly brilliant fellow, often rational, although with delusions of persecution, moderately severe. But that's not uncommon, after all. If there are any acutely paranoiac tendencies, they aren't readily manifest. Certainly a remediable case, no matter what you may hear."

They were approaching the south wing, but Claude, glad to be moving, anywhere, asked Franklin how long Stowe had been with them.

"Twentyeight months," Franklin replied, "and I feel that in this case we've been more than remiss. Bronson should be outside by now. He's certainly remediable." During their walk Franklin had waved amiably to the men they passed, and now entering the south wing he paused here and there to offer friendly greetings, remarks. For the most part the men seemed fond of him. Inside the wing he led Claude to the elevator (which Claude had not known was there) and on the ride up went over again what they might expect of Bronson Stowe. He had little new to add, except that Bronson had had a hellish childhood—although, after all. . . At the fifth floor Franklin took Claude's arm again, directed him along the corridor. Crying could be heard from behind closed doors, but it was not nearly so bad as it had been at night. Almost it seemed that they did not mean it now, were practicing. Franklin stopped at room 531, put his ear to the door before he opened it an inch. "Bronse?" he called. Getting no answer he stepped back to swing the door wide—they all swung toward, as with closets and refrigerators. The room was obviously empty, its chairs were neatly aligned with the wall and no one had sat on either of the beds since they were made, but Franklin went to his knees to peer under them. "Bronse?" he said, and he stood up again. He looked in the closet too, but nobody was behind the clothes. At the window, looking down at the grounds, he spoke apologetically to Claude. "Bronson must be in therapy," he said. "By God, it is Thursday morning, isn't it? Sorry to have led you on such a fruit-less chase. That's my absent-mindedness. I tell you what," he said, stepping to one of the beds and lying down on it, "I'll just wait here until he gets back from therapy, then we'll look for you out on the grounds. I want you to meet Bronse, Claude. Just swing that door to after you . . ."

Claude, swinging the door quietly to, said he would be waiting for them. He had not made up his mind about Franklin yet, Franklin too wore no white uniform. The elevator had gone somewhere, but was empty when it came back for Claude. It was one of the relaxed, sigh-ing ones, going down. He must have pressed the wrong button, or several of them, for when the door fretted open he found himself deep underground, with no heart to try again. The corridor was dark, the air heavy with must, the rooms on both sides quiet yet stirring, as though numb people within were digging themselves out. Thus Claude wasn't much surprised to hear a low cry from one, nor a body thumping against a wall as if head-and-elbows first. He would have kept on, but the door was open a crack. In the bright room he could see the grappling pair, roughly equal in height, but the boy's shoulders and torso massive enough to hide all but the outflung arms of the girl. Now they appeared to be holding one another tensely at rest, and from the doorway Claude could hear them breathe harshly by turns. They did not know he was here.

"Hey in there," Claude called, and the boy looked around. He was young, fifteen at most, but with a man-sized face and a dense white down above his heavy lips. He was dully observant, too calm. Stepping into the room, Claude was conscious of his own slenderness, and the hardness and shine of his new shoes. He said, "What's going on here?" but the boy left his hands on the girl. She too stared out blondly at Claude, smiling a little. Even in crusty white she seemed lax, softly penetrable. "It's all right, I don't mind," she said huskily, smiling still. "Billy's all right." One of her hands reached up to roughen the boy's thick hair. "He's nice," she said, Billy leering at Claude.

"Ah," Claude said. He turned to the door.

"Thanks though," the girl called to his back. "That was nice of you to stop."

"Sure," said Claude closing the door. "See you around."

He found the stairs and climbed them, pushing through to the air. On the front steps he stopped to light a cigarette, paying no heed to the hopeful watchers. Across the ground his men were at morning recreation, but he found himself in no humor for limp volley ball. Instead he took the path along the deserted side of the south wing, the almost deserted side where one man lay spread on his back beneath a tree. A young man Claude had not seen, he lifted his arm from his eyes as Claude came near, looked up at him from the depths of a pale grey face. Claude said hello.

"Feel the pressure," the young man said, covering his eyes again. "It's too much today."

Claude knelt beside him. "You should get up. The ground is wet."

[16]

"No, it's the air, the air," the young man said. "The pressure's too much, eighteen pounds today." He rolled to his side and he was writhing now, snakelike, from the waist. He was crying too. "Do you feel the pressure?" he asked.

"Yes. Come, let's stand up." Claude reached over to roll the young man back, but turned to a strong hand on his arm. "Ah, Father. Hello."

"Don't touch him!" Father Robb said. His dark face smiled briefly, but his hand held pain until Claude had risen stiff at his side. Then he let Claude go. "He doesn't want to be bothered by anything at all," Father Robb said. "I know." He looked broodingly on the boy for a moment before he turned and walked back the way he had come.

Dr. Hemphill was approaching from the north, his stiff long legs carrying him over the ground rapidly enough, although nothing like so well as he seemed to ask. "Who is it?" he called sharply, a few paces out. "Oh, Ronald," he said, as Claude stepped aside.

"I was going to help him up," Claude said, "but Father Robb said he didn't want to be touched."

"The Father's right."

"He seemed to want help . . ."

"The Father's right," Dr. Hemphill repeated. "Father Robb knows." He too stood looking down at the boy before he turned away. Claude left too. The doctor had started fast, as though giving Claude every chance to walk alone, but he had not made himself clear enough. Claude had imagined they were leaving together. They had walked that way for ten paces or so, Claude just behind, when the doctor thrust his hands in his pockets, slowed. He glanced aside at Claude very briefly, just long enough to find something to smile about. "Well, how do you like it?" he asked in his quick way.

"Like it?"

"Yes, the nut house," Dr. Hemphill said. He smiled

[17]

hard at the ground, as if fighting down the urge to see what effect he'd had.

"Well, I can't pretend that I . . ." Claude started, allowing himself to be cut off by the doctor's snigger. He did not like much better his own laugh when he heard it. They walked on, both looking at the ground, both silent, Claude trying to prevent his arms from swinging too freely beside the doctor's, rigidly clamped at his sides. Dr. Hemphill had a way of making anyone else's silence become an untenable mask for pique or stupidity: it was something he did with a slight sidewise tilt of his head. "Doctor," Claude spoke clearly, "I've been wondering about little Ann."

"Little Ann?" said Dr. Hemphill, at once baffled and amused by the name. "Anna Bloutz?"

"I guess so, yes. It's sad to see her spend all her days with those women . . ."

"What *women*?"

"All those big-legged women in their kimonos," Claude threw out, and Dr. Hemphill let it remain hanging there. "But quite aside from such considerations," Claude went on, "isn't it true that most of those women are sick—I mean physically?"

"Sick!" shouted Dr. Hemphill, nearly laughing. "Among them those girls have every damned disease known to man."

"I understand the state has tried to find foster parents for Ann, but they never keep her long?"

"No, she won't have them," the doctor corrected him. "She runs away."

"Runs back here?"

"She usually tries to," Dr. Hemphill said. "She spent the first three years of her life with her mother here, until her mother died. Bleeding ulcers of the bowels," he added, but when Claude gave it no notice: "She was weened, teethed, toilet trained, brought up in this place."

[18]

Claude let that hang too. Then, "Does that mean you've given her up?" he asked.

"We've got nine hundred patients here," was Dr. Hemphill's answer to that, "all disturbed, nutty, sick, what you will, in one way or another. Our job is to work with all of them, return as many of them as we can to what they call a normal life—to put it more succinctly, get them the hell out of here. That's just what we do, as best we can. Without discriminating among them, choosing, neglecting, but simply doing what damn little we can for all."

"If I were doing it," Claude said to him, "I would begin with Ann."

At this the doctor took his hands from his pockets—out of frustration only, not to congratulate. "I don't think I caught your name."

"Claude. Claude Squires."

"What are you, Mr. Squeers, Social Worker III or IV?"

"No, Helper II."

"Oh," Dr. Hemphill said. "Well. I don't have anything at all to do with administration. I'm sorry. You could ask at the office though. There must be openings almost all the time—social workers seem to drop off like flies in here. The exams are held at the Post Office Building, you know. On the fourth floor, in the morning usually, I think. You can check with the office on that . . ."

"No, I don't . . . "

"What's this all about?" the doctor wanted to know, shoving his hands into his pockets again. "Field work for some psychology course? Some sort of term paper you have to turn in?"

No, Claude shook his head.

"Do you think you're getting a little old for that kind of thing? How old *are* you, twentyfive? You'll be thirty soon. Do you think it's time you found yourself a job and went to work somewhere?"

"Doctor, I got the feeling you don't want me here."

Tipping his head the doctor studied him thoughtfully, top to bottom, trying to reach some kind of verdict on him. "You'd better stay on the paths with those shoes," he at last said. "The grass is damp." Then he let his legs carry him quickly off over the lawn. Claude watched him go. When the doctor was as good as gone, a thin walking stick among Siberian elms, Claude headed the other way, with each step he took carefully bruising the grass.

"Hi, Claude!"

She was still by the benches, playing in the circle of dirt uncovered by their feet, and he could not pass her silently by, nor could he call out. He waved. She asked a question of them, but this time they told her no. Two or three pushed on their knees, raising themselves instead. They stood there a moment (there were two) adjusting their straps, then started over the grass toward him, their slippered feet step-stepping very daintily under their robes. The effect was that although they did not own these grounds, they knew very well indeed the people who did. Yet when finally they stopped before Claude, inches away, they smiled almost shyly at him, and stood lifting loose curls of hair from their foreheads. The larger or wider one spoke. "Mr. Claude, we have a friendly favor to ask."

"Yes?"

"It's about our little girl, Mr. Claude."

Priggishly he said, "Anna?"

"We hear they want to send little Ann away again."

"Oh?"

"That's what we hear. But Mr. Claude, you know she wouldn't be happy anywhere else, because she loves it here with us."

"I'm sorry, I have nothing at all to do with that. . ."

"But you could try to explain to them," the woman said. "They talk to you."

"No," he said.

"You could try, Mr. Claude."

"No." He stepped quickly around the pair and veered to the east, past the south wing to the croquet court. Since there was no fence around the grounds he went out in the world in the way of the Bailey boys, straight cross-country, on the run and without goodbye. Gaining the street he slowed for breath, a cigarette, but did not stop. He had no dalliance with the pups, though he doubted that they had lost the scent. Perhaps they were merely better-bred in this neighborhood. He was hurrying north. Here too he might have seen more interesting plant life, had he looked. He knew that a few of the lawns strove for individuality, being made of new materials such as plastics and rocks, but his only pause was at a corner store for a cold six-pack of beer. Mr. Saki looked upon this frivolity in the way a man should who regularly worked fifteen hours: he smiled, bowed, and handed Claude his beer upside down.

Outside he hurried again, for he had several blocks to walk and the beer turned out to be no more than cool. He told himself he would remember next time to deal from the bottom—but the civil sirens sounded, surprising him with his silly private thought. That's what they blow them for. Thought is a national product, issued, like survival, on a day to day basis. There you go. Until tomorrow. When he understood this would be a long one today, he hurried on. As usual, despite all routine precautions, he arrived not quite prepared for her house. How did he forget? Pink, or as she had it, shrimp, it sat square on its plot like a new model tomb wired off from the rest. He had to put his beer on the sidewalk while he opened the trick gate. In the yard her madly pruned trees stood up like two hairy flagpoles on either side of the straight path; the lawn, made with grass, needed his attention again. On the stoop he made sure the key was under the howdy mat before he sorted the mail. His letter this week was a blue one from a girl in Arizona he did not clearly recall. Holding the odorless missive in his teeth he tucked back the rest of the mail (the sirens stopped) and unlocked the front door, stepped into the front room where everything waited religiously in its place, overpolished, unwrinkled, lidded, and racked. All the front windows were blinded and sealed. Even the telephone squatting in its niche by the door helped the four dim brown pictures, one on each wall, lend a hallowed air to the room. But above the bare lookcase the little electric clock fanned its face restively and hummed the time, noon straight up, to the thermostat.

For his part, Claude was up on his toes in the center of the plush carpet before he got hold of himself. Dropping back on his heels he shoved through the swinging door, to the box. Here was one place where she allowed herself to relax, but he made room for his beer by stacking her plastic containers one on another, then her plastic bags upon those. He spun the dial to extra heavy load, opened a tepid can of Lager O-O-O. Returning with it to the barefaced room, he tossed all the pillows in a heap at one end of the couch. Next he lay back on the couch with his head to what light came from the windows, and opened his mail. He read his letter twice, smiling, before he let it drop from his fingers. Vivien James. He remembered her now. She remembered him better. Sighing, closing his eyes after a long hard week at the office, he slipped into a deathlike sleep.

He awoke, to find his body swollen and numb on its back in a room where everything, even the same dead cast of the light, seemed to deny he had slept. He looked everywhere for reassurance and found it in the electric clock, too small and far off to read, yet clearly open-armed. What apparently had awakened him was a throb in its hum. He for his part lay there willingly enough, entirely paralyzed below the neck, taking life with his nerves alone: he had no choice. When finally the blood began to return to an arm and hand, he felt for the cigarettes, then the matches, soon the beer. The beer was warm and, he judged, at least four hours old, but he gulped it down nonetheless, having forgotten to ask Mr. Saki for a guarantee. That done, up on his back with his feet on the floor, he told himself he was ready for anything, even another.

He plunged into the kitchen, the refrigerator, touching home too late in a game of tag with his feet. The beer, frozen solid, thumped heavily against the sides of its can. At the sink he let warm water run over them all for a minute, then opening one ducked his face to a spray of straight alcohol. He carried his can of ice into the front room and left it melting on the television set, which he turned low to an unoccupied channel. Lying down on the couch, he read his letter again while he waited. This time he did not smile very much, but found himself instead a little annoyed by its sprightly-intellectual tone and her obvious assurance that he would be flattered. For instance, he could not imagine why she still thought of him every time a plane shattered the sound barrier, or why she listened with her other, undeafened ear to the movie gossipers for lurid news of his doings. But she wasn't really that bad. He remembered that much.

He got up to take his beer from the television, put another one on. This week's magazines, all five of them, lay pokered out on the table according to size, there being no other easy distinction. He chose the largest and carried it back to the couch. Since the army he had made a snobbish point of avoiding these things, thus it fascinated him to learn all that had happened lately up in the world. He devoured this big one ravenously, went back for another, another, another: almost he was sorry to hear her key in the door. She had brought her bright smile home from the office, but she quickly lost it at full sight of her room and him in it. Even so she did not appear angry, simply a little confused as she might if the boss shat on her typewriter. "Hello, Claudine."

She did not answer but placed her mail on the table on her way to the kitchen with the groceries, nor did she speak at once upon her return. She went first to the television. He felt instant pity for her when she turned to face him, that awkward can of beer in her hand; but she said "Claude," and he smiled.

"That's yours, Claudine," he said, "unless you'd like me to get you a cold one."

"No. I have to change."

"All right, I'll take it." He stood up and went over to her, bent to kiss her pale cheek. Always he was stunned by the softness of it, even compared to the others he knew. He reminded himself that this was merely a calculated process, cunningly made up and served daily to brutalize men. Yet he remembered his surprise twenty years ago too. He went to the sink for warm water.

"Claude, do you know where Darlise is?"

"She's probably over at Mary's."

"Which Mary's?"

"Mary Mary's," he said, and Claudine did slam the door.

When he returned to the front room she had the pillows arranged, herself arranged on an end one, with her long black hair spread out at rest on the back of the couch, her dainty slippers dangling free of the slipcover, all of her slim body coiled tensely between, reading her mail. She had changed into a pale blue lounging robe, perfectly spotless, buttoned at the neck and pinched together in front by the clenched hand in her pocket. He felt, although he could not say positively, that few men would be tempted to open that robe. Most would be leery of finding something unprecedented, like scale, inside. He was one of only two or three who knew better, which seemed shameful to him, and hopeless. In fact, he had given her up. There was a time when she could have been a real French pastry of a girl, with that kind of variety, but she had had two semesters at St. Bernard. She had had other things too. Some of them he had had himself. She asked, "How are you?"

"Oh fine. And you?"

"Fine."

For a moment he drank beer while she played pat-a-cake with one of her slippers.

"I see you got some mail."

"Oh yes."

"Do I know her?"

"No, it's just a fan letter."

Her toes curled in a smile. "Then there's some other explanation why you're here so early."

"Yes."

"Don't tell me they gave you a day off."

"No, I took one."

"Oh," she said, quietly pat-a-caking, "is this permanent?"

"Yes."

"Did something happen?"

"What does *that* mean?"

"It means exactly what I said, did something happen today?"

"Good God," he said, on his feet. "Something happens every minute, every second, Claudine."

"Did you get fired?"

"Not exactly."

"Claude, let me ask you, what did they say?"

"They said the grass was too wet for me," he said, and went after a beer although he was not ready. By the time he came back she had thought of a more discouraging question.

"Let me ask you, what are you going to do now, Claude?"

"I don't know." He stood with his back to Claudine,

warming his beer with his hands and studying one of her brown pictures. It was one of the kind that for unimaginable reasons strive to look like photographs taken by a commercial photographer twenty centuries ago, the beautiful face retouched and made pretty, the skin of the hands unwrinkled, effeminate, the robe like Claudine's, terribly clean. In effect it was the photo of a dead man.

"Is that all you have to say?"

"I don't know. Ask me questions."

In the moment of silence that followed he could hear the pat-pat of her slipper. "Do you think you can afford to sit around and drink beer for the rest of your life?"

"No," he said. "Only a year or two."

"Oh, I give up!"

He turned to see her twisted sidewise away from him, lifting her hair up so that she could rest her heavy head on her hand. "Well, what are you waiting for," he wanted to know of her, leaning forward and speaking loudly. "What would you like me to do, try the kennels and the mortuaries? I've tried the hotels. Maybe I should go back to them, tell them I've had experience now, seven and a half days in the nut house. Hey, maybe I could get room and board at the morgue. . . No, on second thought, I think I'll go back to school and study embalming."

Claudine flicked that aside with her hair. "Didn't you learn anything in all those schools you went to in the army?"

Now it almost seemed she too had lost the joy of fruitless argument. But she said, "There's always Daddy."

"Oh God, please, please stop, Claudine," he said, standing over her. "Please?"

"What's the matter, Claude?" she asked. "Can't you even talk any more?"

"We aren't talking!"

Staring at her wriggling toes, she did stop a minute. "I was only trying to think about your future. Somebody has to."

"O. K., thanks very much," he said as he drank beer from both of his cans. "I don't know, maybe I'll get married."

Uncoiling she laughed, laughed again plumping the pillows. "That will be the day," she said.

"Oh, won't it."

The doorbell rang and Claudine left him standing still, so he sat down. Before she blocked his view he had a glimpse of the stocky bespectacled man in his tidy black uniform, the square military set of his shoulders, the little plastic lid that protected his fancy braided cap from the sprinklers and birds. He was already speaking: "Pacific Missionaries Army, ma'am. Your dollar sends a Bible overseas, places a Bible in the home that doesn't have one. Your dollar helps spread the word of God at home and abroad." He had a beautiful voice which he spat out in a rhythmic, narcotic chant that made the listener almost want to hear more: "Your dollar helps God's love enter into the hearts and minds of men."

Claudine had switched on a light to better read the plastic card she found in her hand. It had a passport-size photo on it, perhaps even a thumbprint, and a new dollar bill was clipped to the back. A fine, gold-mesh bag protected the card, and the dollar. "Oh, you're Carl, aren't you," said Claudine. "I've heard Stanley Rogers speak of you on his program. . ."

"Carl Arnold, ma'am, Pacific Missionaries Army."

"Yes, I remember seeing your picture on television. I listen to Brother Stan every week without fail—he's a wonderful man, doing so much good work for the world. Are you twice born?"

"Twice born, ma'am. Your dollar sends a Bible overseas, places a Bible in the home that doesn't have one."

"God bless you. I've been wondering," Claudine said,

"I have three Bibles. Do you accept used Bibles?"

"What you can, ma'am. Your dollar helps spread His message at home and abroad."

"Well, let me ask you, do you distribute Bibles of all denominations?"

"Headquarters will answer any questions you may have, ma'am. The number is there on the card. What you can."

"Well, you see," Claudine said, twisting the door handle, "our church is constructing a new auditorium. . ."

"What you can."

"To be perfectly honest with you, I don't know that I have a cent in the house. You see, I stopped at the grocery store on my way home from work and I just now got home. . ."

"What you can."

"Well, I'm afraid. . ." Claudine looked back into the room over her shoulder.

"What you can."

"Let me look," she said, and on her way to the bedroom she glanced with real cruelty at Claude, at his two beers, one in the hand and one in the plush. Carl Arnold looked at them too. Claude could tell by the direct gleam of his spectacles. Beneath the square chin, above the tight collar, the muscular throat swallowed loudly.

"Twice born?" Claude called.

"Twice born."

Together they listened to Claudine's return, Carl Arnold's shoulders squaring to her crackling dollar.

"I had to take this from my little girl's purse!"

Carl Arnold had his hand ready. "Whatyoucan," he said, taking the dollar. He asked Claudine her name and address, wrote out her receipt quickly, slipped it quickly through the crack of the screen door. Then he tucked Darlise's dollar in his wallet and left. Claudine was leaning against the doorjamb now, and Claude could see how deftly Carl Arnold opened the trick gate and, not looking back, closed it behind him. Claudine stood watching him go, her diligent fingers latching and unlatching the screen. "God bless you!" she called.

"Go to hell," called Claude.

Closing the door, Claudine looked at him. She looked at him, and while he waited for some expression to come to her face he knew how a doctor must feel sometimes when he looks at a belly. For her face was no more than a cover of skin, showing nothing of the terrible, complicated things, ugly and beautiful, that were going on inside her. It was as though he alone knew, of the two of them. At most hers was a vicarious knowledge, gathered from old books and pictures. All she knew was the pain, and the flesh could not express that. She did not try words, if she had any. Stuffing her receipt in her pocket, she ran to the kitchen. Her pain, being purely subjective, did not concern him, but out of deference to it he did not go in there except after beer, and Claudine did not come into the front room until Darlise returned from Mary Mary's.

They entered at the same time through their opposite doors. Meeting in the center of the room they held their cheeks against one another much too long, like dolls made to kiss by a child. When at last they backed off, Claudine said, "Hurry, you're late. . ."

"Hello, Uncle Claude."

"And you didn't change out of your school clothes."

"Uncle was sleeping."

"You heard me, hurry, Darlise."

They left as they had entered, simultaneously pushing through doors, but Claudine was back in a moment to peer palely into the front room for someone forgotten.

"Have you eaten today?"

"I had breakfast at home."

"Ugh. Come eat your dinner."

"I'm not hungry."

He was dismayed to find his six-pack all gone, he usually counted. Claudine set a big glass of ice water in front of him, beside coffee, like the hot and cold baths at the office. For dinner she had prepared her little wet meatballs drenched in lemon juice, turgidly called by her Koenigsberger Klops, but nonetheless delicious. Ravenous, he sent them down quickly to quiet the burbling O-O-O in his stomach, and to spare himself watching Darlise's painstaking progress. Her way was to begin with her nearest serving and eat every bite of that before tackling her next, so on across her big plate. It looked like a game, but it was not that imaginative. Neither did Darlise speak while she ate—it was a discipline imposed on her by Claudine in lieu and lack of a father. The two ate in silence, watching one another over their food, but each ready to raise a finger to her lips if the other started to say something, as though they listened all the while to a very detailed account of today at the office. Ordinarily Claude found their manners deplorable, but tonight he was grateful. As soon as he had finished his klops he went to the livingroom, Claudine following.

"Let me ask you, have you thought any more about what you will do?"

"No. Have you heard from Mother."

"No."

He went to the couch for his letter, on an impulse leaving the envelope there. "Who knows," he said, "maybe I'll go to Arizona."

"Arizona? Why Arizona?"

"Why California?"

For a moment it seemed that was all they would say, they had done well to find that much. In the past they had parted from too many people, most often together. But remembering those days he couldn't leave her with nothing, as though he had already forgotten her. "You know that guy I was telling you about at the office? Franklin Storrs? I don't think you'd be interested. . ."

"I don't either."

"I mean I talked to him again today. . ."

"Don't worry about me," Claudine said. "If you want to worry about someone, worry about that poor little farmer's daughter you're going to."

"She's not like that."

"Isn't she?"

"No," he said, opening the door.

"Well whatever she's like, I feel sorry for her."

"So do I," he said, nibbling soft cheek of mushroom as he slid past her.

"Are you crazy?"

"So long, Darlise."

"Goodbye, Uncle!"

Claudine stood desolately watching him, without blessings, punishing him with silent beatitudes instead. At the trick gate he waved to her, and she waved back. He moved quickly under the streetlamp, wondering if she too was thinking that this might be the last time she would see him. He doubted it, but nevertheless he carried his unhappiness as unobtrusively as possible, not hiding it but carrying it before him as though he were leaving a store with something he had bought in another store earlier, before he remembered they also carried it here. When he heard her door close he knew he was in darkness. Twenty years ago he would have cried for them both.

He had thought to pay Mr. Saki a visit, but at sight of the store he found himself uninvited. In truth he was not feeling very well, and at the corner he took a turn for the worse, heading into the city. Now the pups padded past him in packs, all leaving. The people at first were gathered on their lawns in dim family clusters, but the farther he went the more they broke up. Soon he was in a block of locked buildings with three boys trotting toward him abreast in the middle of the street. They passed him by. Before the Gay Peacock an old lady with dark red hair was perched on her heels discussing the future with an earnest young man in a softdrink uniform. Now it was settled and he led her firmly away by the elbow, anxious to do his good turn for tonight. At the highschool a pretty girl strolled across the parking lot to her black stallion, let her cigarette dangle from her lips while she put on her helmet, adjusted her goggles. Throwing a slender white leg over the side she jacked her little backside up and down a few times, exciting the steed. Now she came down on his back and he squatted, moaning to the soft squeeze of her hand, then at her sudden clutch shot out fast between the press of her knees. Claude looked down at his shoes as they passed, having seen nothing. But he glanced up in time to watch them glide off under the next streetlamp, the gleaming beast appearing almost languid with release, very pleased with himself and with the girl who clung to his back small and stiff and unsatisfied.

She had been noticed: everywhere along the way the leaning people looked after her as though wondering if the new week had finally begun, then they looked at one another, then back at nothing. In the main they ignored Claude, but a few did glance up at him hopefully, the very bored ones. Of these the wise majority said no, some said nothing, one or two, notably a short-legged girl dark in a white sweater, said why not? Claude, caring for none of this now, walked on until he came to the largest neon sign in the city, red and purple, in the form of a cat, with his name on it. He turned in past the boys never too busy to deal him a smile, past the rows of ten dollar bills under the wipers, stopping by the little English roadster that said "Guess my price and you can have me" just long enough to scribble the answer (£798 /6) and sign it not for himself but for Franklin Storrs, in care of the office. At the little white sales shack the folding chairs were tipped back against the front wall but unoccupied, the door generously open to nothing.

In the shack he paused before the door marked private long enough to place his facial muscles under rigid control, but even as he entered he knew he could not maintain it. For they, in their smiles and their shiny suits and their suntans and their generous stances, borrowing the illusion of unusual size from the sheer bulk of them together in this low-ceilinged room, swung as one to overwhelm him, like a team of all-American fatties welcoming a fan come to help them celebrate the start of the season. The centermost of them lumbered forward to press Claude's hand firmly (all their muscle was in their right hands) but the rest of the line, not qu-ite making it, leaned and/or sat where they smiled, waving or lifting their highball glasses in greeting. To one side, on the bench, lay their cheerleader Carlotta, flanked by some of the biggest backs and ends in the game. And over at the bar their coach, affectionately known as the Cat, squatted on a stool discussing the new plays with his co-captains. Crossing the red carpet Claude could almost believe he passed among buddies, not a few of whom had never seen him before, which was what finally made him lose all control. "Hi," he said, grinning, and the Cat himself sprang from his stool waving him forward.

"Come on in, pal."

He was still the prettiest one of them all. Even surrounded by the younger generation he looked big, if no longer tremendous, his shiny coat seemed to fit him more honestly than theirs for having been worn longer, and his long pants were full but not bursting with baby-fat. He had the further advantage that his smile wrinkles were burnt indelibly into his face, so that at those odd moments when he was not using them they served as deep white furrows of character. Topping all this was a sterling crown of tight curls, hand-wrought, highly polished, worn casually. As a boy Claude had feared that given all these graces, plus his talent for meeting only the big men in the whirl and knowing them by name without knowing them, the Cat would someday be President, but he need not have worried. The Cat was too fond of his milk to be truly carnivorous, and the Cat knew it. That was why he spent his nights in the clubhouse with the boys, plotting his cunning plays, and flexing his smile muscles. That was why he leaned a little too far over the bar to offer his son what he could, a strong right hand and a jocular "Pal, let me pour you a saucer."

Seated beside the co-captains, his belly softly O-O-O-ing, Claude watched the Cat lace a large bowl of cognac with white creme de menthe, tenderly stir it. It was the Cat's favorite drink and he served it to Claude as a matter of course, as one of the family. He had made more than enough for them both, and now he brushed around the bar to claim his share. "Stay where you are, boys," he said, and the co-captains vanished. Making a gymnasium for himself of their stools, the Cat hunched forward to drink. When he had had all he wanted he reached intricately through rungs for a handkerchief and, still bent over, wiped his damp lips. Now sitting up straight he tucked the handkerchief into his breast pocket, stretched one arm out full-length on the bar, the other to the back of Claude's stool. "O.K., pal," he said, "tell me the latest."

"Well . . . " Claude felt for his cigarettes. For an instant the Cat crouched as though expecting a slap on the nose, but he quickly thrust the cigarette between his lips with the hand from the bar, whipped out his lighter and offered flame too with that hand. "Where did we leave off last time?" Claude asked.

The Cat was stretched out again, his head tilted slightly back and aside to look past smoke at Claude.

"How have you been, pal? Still working for that paper?"

"No."

"What was the matter, not enough honey?"

"No, that part was all right."

"They work you too hard?"

"Not that either. We didn't get along well, to put it some way."

"Anything serious? I could speak to someone."

"Don't do it," Claude said, the Cat drawing back from his voice.

"Hell, I'll cancel my ad if the bastards are that bad."

Claude smiled. 'Let me put it another way—I don't like what they print in their paper."

"Ah, the news," said the Cat, the lines in his face showing very white as he looked down at the bar. "Nobody likes it."

"They don't print it."

"Oh?" The Cat watched Claude uneasily now, seemed to wait for him to continue, but nothing happening he moved over to drink, suddenly bored with their game. His thirst turned out to be real. When he straightened up it was as though he had forgotten what they had been playing, or hoped Claude had forgotten. "What are you doing now, pal?"

"Nothing right now."

"Well then . . ."

"Well no." It was Claude's turn to drink, not very long. He looked up to see the Cat drop the end of his cigarette carefully into the ash tray, smother it with what seemed an excessive fastidiousness, especially in view of the sudden indifference with which he turned his back to it.

"Speaking of intra-office problems, I've had a few unfortunate experiences in the matter of personnel myself recently. I don't know, these always seem to come periodically, cyclically." Speaking he sat forward and tense on his stools, rather wide-eyed, rolling his big words out before him too deliberately and pausing to look after them too often, as though waiting to be asked for a translation. There seemed also a new quality in his voice, a new roundness, or perhaps Claude had simply been too young or near to notice all this when they lived together. Here at the bar they smiled almost bashfully at one another for a moment. But the Cat could speak in several voices, and the one he chose now suited him better: "I had to ditch one of the boys just tonight, a few minutes before you came in. God knows I didn't want to do it, I kept him on longer than I should have, gave him every chance in the world to make good, but what he did was sit around in here boozing all day and then go out at night and cream one of my cars. It got so he was creaming more cars than he sold." Did you give him his commission on the insurance? "Hell, there was a day when if I had an opening all I had to do was snap my fingers and twenty good boys would come running— I mean real class, real beauties—but now . . . " Now fatties? "I don't know what's the matter with the boys nowadays, whether they're getting soft or what. I give them a nice clean job with plenty of you-know, but they don't seem to show their appreciation. They don't want to work for their honey any more, they want alimony." Have you sent Mother her check lately? "I don't know," he said, frowning. "Maybe it's me, Claude . . . Claude, did you ever look at a tree in the forest?" No, never. "I mean a big old tree long past its prime, so old that you said to yourself, 'If I had an ax with me I'd chop that tree down'?" Hardly ever. " 'All that old tree is good for is casting shade and getting in the way of the others'?" Let's leave it. "Let's face it, Claude—I'm not getting any younger. I guess you know I'll be fifty next month?" He looked expectantly at Claude, and Claude gave him a big smile for his birthday. "O.K., enough of this sad talk. I don't like to be pessimistic, especially with you, pal," he said, cuffing

[36]

Claude's shoulder. "I know I've been lucky. By that I don't mean to say I haven't earned every damned thing I've got—you could say that every car out there on the lot represents a good year of my life." Come now, how old *are* you? "Well, six months of my life, call it. Put that way, it makes you pause and think, doesn't it?" The Cat paused, but Claude could think of nothing. "I don't kid myself, a man doesn't put on this much fat all by himself," he needs plenty of mice. "He needs Guidance. 'The Lord giveth the power to get wealthy.' Maybe this trouble I've been having is just the Lord's way of reminding me that nothing in this world comes easy. Maybe I've had so many good boys all the way that He sent along a few bums, or poets, to show me how bad it can be."

"You seem to have a full, well-rounded team here tonight," Claude said, while the Cat bent to pour from the bowl.

"Oh sure, these are good boys," the Cat said, looking them over. He had a gadget above the bar that buzzed whenever a car door was opened in the ordinary way, by the ignorant public (salesmen opened them quickly, without touching any other part of the car); each time the buzzer sounded one of the team would peel off, rest his drink on the table or bar, and slip quietly out the door combing his hair. A few minutes later he would come back smiling to himself, combing his hair, shaking his head in bemusement at what he had seen out there. He was a good boy. "These are all good boys," the Cat said. There were no individual stars on this team: each played his part with the minutest possible deviations from all the others, visible only to experts. Thus most spectators were bored, although it did not seem to keep them away. "That one that just came in—Harry?" Sure, I know Harry Halfenback. "He works down at the C of C—" chamber of conners. "This one in the tan suit, Eddie," Eddie Fullerback, "is employed at First Trust—" oh, anyone can tell. "Elwood there is studying for his real estate exam . . . " Well! "That big one, Clay There, is a deputy sheriff,"—mind if I pass? "A good half of the boys have other jobs during the day, come over here five-six nights a week. I guess they represent just about every field you can name." Insurance. "Insurance, investment, real estate, radio-television . . . " I guess that about covers it. "Food supplements. I even had a highschool teacher this winter—a real sharp boy he was too—but he had to go back home . . . " Hell. "Arkansas, I think. I'd say nine out of ten of these fellows," ten out of eleven, "have been to college or business school. But there're still a few tricks they can learn from the Cat, that's why they're here. It's a real pleasure to teach boys like these. They look up to me as a father image, and I don't mind telling you I get a bang out of it. I'd be proud to have any one of these boys as my son." Could we arrange a quick deal—say you take Harry Halfenback there, I'll take that little English job you're giving away? "Claude," the Cat said, "when these boys go home tonight they'll be able to look Him right in the eye and say, 'Well Lord, I'm a little bit bigger man than I was yesterday,' and believe me that's one of the best feelings there is in the world."

Claude, who had been playing with his drink, found himself suicidally lapping it now, slobbering, "Where do most of them put up, at the Y?"

"Clown, these boys are family men. I like to hire family men, and I make it a point to visit each of them with their families, in their homes. They've got the nicest little wives in the world, a real bunch of dolls, and I'd say they average already three-four kids apiece, more on the way . . . " Who in hell do they get to do it for them? I mean even if they found the time, wouldn't it be a strain on their muscles? These are the kind of boys that carry their kids in the back of their pants, where they can exhibit them better. These are nice boys, well-mannered, with a well-rounded recreational program that leaves them no time or energy to play around with the girls. These boys aren't layers. They aren't cocks either, they're pullets. Harry there is a capon. I suppose there must be a few breeders still around, and if so you can bet these boys know where to find them. They have little blue books in their pockets that give them the whole picture, list price according to style, make, and year, standard equipment or fancy. You know they get their proper commission. Do they watch? Or is that what they're all grinning about, giving themselves a little twiddle with imagining the doll at home on her back, some other wild posture, getting a good pecking at this very minute? " . . . family men, Claude."

"Then why aren't they home with their families?"

"You haven't been listening to me, Claude. It takes lots of honey to raise a family these days . . . " No, it isn't even that, these teddy bears don't like honey as much as they think they do. They think they're supposed to like it, the way they're supposed to like women and children. They think they're supposed to act like real grizzlies, but they don't feel it. You can't blame them, they just don't have it inside them. What they have, what they love most, is their memories: how the Coach used to shout niceworkpal whenever they caught the big ball or somehow hit the little one, how Dad used to wink when they caught one of his jokes, how when they repeated them he almost died laughing, so they told them and told them—if they told one really well he might do it. They memorized all the conversations verbatim, that about the pussies and the coons, the homers and the balls, the cams and the bearings. They're still memorizing. You can see them almost anytime you're out driving, there in the slow car just ahead, the young man at the wheel, the old man talking, the young man leaning a little to the right in order to hear better, the old man pointing out the properties, the young man looking and listening earnestly, straining to catch the old man's last word, the last joke verbatim, the last bit of know-how about the deals and the properties and the honey. When he thinks he's learned all he can from the old man, he'll shove him out of the car. You watch, next time you're out driving. " . . . these are the cream, Claude." These are the all-American fairies.

"I had supper at Claudine's tonight, Dad."

His father was behind the bar mixing a bowl, and Claude watched how tenderly he stirred it, how exactly he placed it between them before he came back to his stools. This time he waited until he was comfortably seated and sated before he stretched his arm behind Claude. "How is Claudine, pal?"

"She's about the same as ever."

"I've been meaning to go over some evening," his father said, hitching one pantleg at the knee with his free hand. "I'd like to see more of her. I don't know what it is, maturity, senility, or what, but I find that I've been bitten by the religious bug myself lately."

"I thought I had noticed something."

"Don't laugh," and Claude felt the palsie cuff on his neck. "This isn't the mushy kind, you know me better than that. This is the straight stuff, Claude. What we do is send Bibles overseas, place Bibles in the homes that don't have them . . . Are you laughing?"

Claude, over his saucer, shook his head wretchedly, to show the Cat that he wasn't. "Go see her," he begged. "She'll be pleased."

Now the Cat took his hand from Claude's back, flicked it out of its long sleeve to look at his watch. "Oh-oh," he said, and bent down to drink. Quickly finishing what there was, he shook his head while wiping his lips. "Pal," he said, chucking him, tucking his handkerchief, "I'm due on the air in a minute to show off a few of our specials. Why don't you take a turn on the lot while I'm gone, give yourself a chance to put on a little fat. I'll speak to Harry." He gave Claude a last big one as he hopped off his stool.

"I won't do it," Claude called, but the Cat was already across the room speaking to Harry, and Harry Halfenback was already nodding his head, looking sharply at Claude, and smiling generously. That settled, the Cat chucked Harry Halfenback's arm. "Come on, Princess," he called to the bench, and Carlotta bounced up. She was wide like the rest of them, but no man could fairly say she was too wide. The most that could be said was that she did not have much further to go before she would have to start squeezing it in and strapping it up, which she clearly did not do now. She let it hang where it was, and it did very nicely by itself. As she passed among the boys they looked her over with unconcealed envy, as though they knew she had something they didn't have but were not quite sure what it was. One thing was certain, she got more exercise than they did.

The next to be noticed were her braids, they hung forward over her terrain, ignoring as much as possible her contours, like two shiny black meridianal lines demarking her longitudes as far down as the equator. It was not hard to imagine oneself spending a long lifetime on that bare little island alone, with no plan or ambition, too overcome with the heat to continue on south to the pole, far less return to the continents. Nothing productive could ever be accomplished there, but there would be comfort such as few men have known, there would be torpor. The body swelled with such thoughts, the mind shrank from them, and the longing eyes traveled finally up north, to where those meridians came together at a point above a bland white area vaguely charted, with few landmarks, no doubt sparsely inhabited. Here the imagination halted.

Her mouth was positively a mouth and no more, neither ruby nor rosebud nor dormant volcano. Her eyes might have been anyone else's somewhat over-exposed. She had the ears and the nose. People said she looked like an Indian princess, and it was not hard to see her that way, Pocahontas of the jigsaw puzzle, a nighttime scene, her full skirt blending unfairly with the black of the lake and the green-black of the forest, her pebbly toes easy to find, her hands also obvious, her head, like the moon, a round piece, in this case somewhat pointed on top. Once Claude had looked forward to seeing one of her pictures on television, but by the time he thought of it again the Cat himself dared no longer present them. It did not matter, he believed he knew pretty well how she did it. There are actresses who learn their first entrance so thoroughly that it does no good to write them new ones, which is not to say that the first was not worth writing.

"Princess, you remember your line?"

The Cat and Princess stood at the mirror, where she now wrung her hands low down before her with such ecstasy that her braids were caught together in the plump pinch of her elbows, her eye shadows sprang up, and her mouth became suddenly a round mouth. The attitude was not subtle, but very very genial. "Ooooh, what a big one," she cried, and, "Will you give it to me, Daddy?"

Grinning at the mirror, the Cat chucked her behind. "You've been practicing."

She curtsied, the Cat bowed to the mirror. Encircling her with an arm, boldly landing on her island, he led her onstage waving and smiling aside all offers of luck. They would not need it, they had a dumb audience. Claude, afloat on his stool through all this, had drunk more milk than he realized. He was laughing. Even so he would have poured himself another but for the sudden call of the buzzer and Harry Halfenback's quick o-k-pal grin. Landing on his feet on the carpet, he made a kind of way through the boys. They all smiled, but nobody wished him good luck as he slipped out the door without combing his hair.

He spotted his mice at once, at a green one not far from the shack, for these were country mice who went directly to whatever they liked without snuffing everything else on the way. He was seated inside with one leg outside, she standing close by clutching her pocketbook. He showed her the gearshift, which seemed to impress her. Now he showed her the radio and the bounce of the cushions, but she only muttered, for she had observed Claude's approach. The man heaved himself out, and she bent stiffly forward to brush at a spot on his shirtsleeve. Looking down at his arm he shrugged her off, looked up grinning slyly at Claude. Claude nodded. They stood facing the green car for a moment, she brushing hard at that spot again. Now she tucked her pocketbook under her arm, held the material taut with one hand while she brushed with the other. She scratched with her fingernail next. That was grease.

"How much is this one?" she asked, looking at Claude, the man looking with sly embarrassment at Claude's ear.

"Doesn't it say on the ticket?"

The man said, "I couldn't find it there nowhere."

They both looked inside, neither finding it there. Then they got out and walked slowly around the car together, the woman following them.

"Does that ten dollar bill come with the car?"

Nodding, Claude lifted the wiper and picked at the bill stuck to the glass with cement.

"Hey, I'd like to be here some night when it's raining," the man said, his wife cackling at that.

Claude took them around back to show them the trunk. It was locked, so he went up front for the key. He held the trunk door for them while they peered inside.

"I don't see no spare in there," the man said.

Claude bent to look too. He held the door up and felt on both sides, but there was no spare to be found. He stood back so the woman could look for herself.

"Maybe we better try another one," the man suggested.

They chose another green one, and the man got inside to feel the gearshift and the bounce of the cushions. Finally he thought to glance at the ticket, his wife too looking as well as she could over his shoulder; but this time they did not ask Claude for clarification. He got the trunk key and led the way around to the back, held the door high.

"Let's try another one," the man said.

They found a green-and-white one this time, and then another a little farther down the line, but after that they began looking at just any car they came to, Claude letting them open the doors, and opening them once more himself with both hands when he went after the trunk keys. At the end of the lot, the man turned to look back down the long row they had tilled.

"I guess we want to shop around before we decide, Mom?"

"Yes."

The man gave Claude a friendly little smile and wave. "We'll probably be back."

"Pleasure to have you," Claude said, waving farewell.

By now the entire team was out on the field hunting for mice; Claude, finding himself no longer needed, slunk around the sales shack to catch the end of the act. He arrived just in time to see the Princess muff her line, stare sullenly at each camera by turn, lift her hands in a knot to her mouth and then drop them as quickly back to her lap, fold suddenly forward so far that each braid became a shaky exclamation point to each hysterical breast. The Cat was delighted. He stood with one hand low, palm up beside a braid, gave each camera a full minute's shrug, a smile both candid and askance. They were standing so, the Cat trying to decide what attitude to assume next, the Princess no doubt getting a cramp in her back and surely a chafe up in front, when the Cat spotted Claude. "Folks," he said loudly, raising his hands over his head, "boys and girls, I know you're anxious to get back to the show, see what happens in that next reel, but I beg your indulgence just long enough to introduce to you another member of the Cat family. He's talented too. Would you like to meet him? Thanks, folks. Come on, pal. Come right up here, son. Come say hello to the folks . . ."

The Princess had remained folded, but now she straightened herself to look with the Cat past the cameras for Claude, smile enthusiastically at him. "No!" he said. He would not do it, of course, no matter what, and he shook his head fiercely at the Cat's palsie wave, his "Come on up, pal. Come say hello." He would not, would not do it, and he was still shaking his head as he stumbled among wires to the beckoning hand, the pleading, "Come on up, son," the almost humble supplication of his father's smile . . .

"That a boy. Stand right here, pal." The Cat put his arm around Claude, which was well, for he found himself leaning dangerously toward the cameras and he dared not lean back. "Folks, this is my youngest," the Cat said, tipping his head to look up at Claude. He did not have to look far. "Claude Junior is a veteran of three years in the service, eighteen months overseas, and now he's through with his college and about ready to make his way in the world. He's been out on the lot tonight getting acquainted with a few of you nice folks who've dropped by to see us. . . . Well, son," he said, tilting to attract Claude's attention, firm his back, "have you been doing any good tonight?"

"No."

"NO? You mean you didn't send that last party away with a new used car?"

[45]

"No."

"Well, son, suppose you tell the Cat all about it, and maybe he can give you a few pointers. What kind of a car were they interested in?"

"A green one."

"A green one," the Cat said, patting Claude proudly, but showing the audience his utter stupification, chagrin. "Did they find a green one they liked?"

"They said they wanted to shop around first."

"Shop around where!"

"They didn't mention."

"Did they say they'd be back?"

"They said so."

"Good boy," the Cat said. "Here's a hundred for your trouble," he said, handing Claude a bill with his right hand and reaching around him to take it back with his left. "You can have that when they come back." He winked at the cameras. "The mice always come back to Claude the Cat. Folks, you watch, the next time you see this boy he'll be wearing a suit. He already has a nice pair of shoes. Boys, give the folks a peek at those shoes," he said to the cameramen, and the cameras dove to Claude's feet. "You can see that this boy is starting at the bottom and working his way up—pretty soon he's going to buy him a belt to hold up those pants," the Cat said, the cameras creeping up to stare at Claude's crotch. "Then one day he'll get him a tie," and the cameras prodded Claude's throat. "No, folks, the next time you see this boy you won't hardly recognize him. Will they, son?"

The cameras glared Claude straight in the eyes. "I hope not," he said, closing them.

"Princess," the Cat called to the Princess. "Come here, Princess. How about giving this boy a little you-know for his trouble."

The Princess went at once into handwrung ecstasy. This time she wrung so thoroughly that it was easy to picture beneath her full skirt the plump knees pinched together in exact imitation of her elbows, though of course clasping no braids. "Oooh, what a big one!" she cried flawlessly. "Will you give him to me, Daddy?" She rose to her toes before Claude, the Cat steadying him, and settled her round mouth over his. "Mmmm," she said, resting one hand on each of Claude's cheeks and drawing him down to her level, by suction. The Cat watched them a moment, and then he looked at the cameras. "That's fine, Princess." He tapped her on the shoulder, but shrugged reassuringly at the cameras when she did not respond. "It's all right folks, she's his stepmother." He was perspiring; they were all perspiring. "There, that'll do fine, Princess. . . . Folks, why don't you come down and get in on the party. Oow, we've got some big ones . . . Princess . . . Boys, turn out those lights!"

The lights did seem to blink out. When they were glaring again the Cat had his supporting players firmly in hand, one at each side, and he was bowing. Now he released them; the cameras had swung for a shot of his big red-purple sign.

"Hey, son, come here. . . . Where are you going?"

"I'll see you." Wiping his face with a sleeve he stumbled among cars like a blind mouse in a playroom.

"Hey . . . Come back here, pal. I've got something for you!" The Cat was blind too, he could hear him painfully thrashing and thumping behind him. "Son . . . Stop a minute!"

He drew up against a fender and waited for the Cat to catch up with him. At first his father too leaned against the fender, panting, then he pushed himself straight, brushing his trousers, shaking his head as he peered at Claude in the gaudy dimness. "Where the hell were you going in such a hurry?"

"Home. I'm tired."

"No hard feelings?"

"Don't worry."

"You could have waited a minute," his father said, still breathing heavily. "I wanted to give you this hundred."

"No, I don't want it . . . " It was in his shirt pocket.

"You earned it, keep it. That was the best show we've put on since we started."

"No, I . . . "

"Shut up," his father said, tucking the bill back in Claude's shirt. "Will I see you tomorrow?"

"That's what I came over to tell you. I'm going to Arizona."

"Arizona!" The Cat had heard of the place. "You got a job out there or something?"

"No."

"What's out there then, a girl?"

He did not think his father could see his face in this shadow.

"Who is she?"

"You don't know her."

"Hell, if that's all it is . . . "

"Let's skip it."

"Hell, we can fix you up here. Your stepmother knows plenty of girls, nice ones . . . "

"Let's drop it."

"Well, Arizona," his father said, wiping his face with a handkerchief. "How were you thinking of getting out there?"

"I was thinking of driving."

"You're in the market for a car?" asked the Cat, tucking his handkerchief.

"I was hoping I could make one of your deliveries."

"Ah. Well," the Cat said, "I hardly ever have one going to Arizona . . . "

They were walking toward the sales shack now. "Anything out in that direction?"

"I don't have more than two-three going out to Arizona a year."

"Any in that general direction?"

"Well, I might have one to Okla City . . ."

"What you can."

Claude followed the Cat toward the sales shack, stopping just long enough to slip the hundred under the wiper of a green one. The Cat met him at the door with a little card in his hand. "Ya, I've got a '59 Thunderhead going to Okla City for a lady."

"I don't suppose she'd mind if I stopped off along the way for a few days."

The Cat thought about this, studied the card. "Why should she care? You'll be buying the gas," he said finally.

"O.K. What kind of A-1 shape is this beast in?"

"You don't care, you aren't buying her."

"Well, let's take a look."

"She's around back," the Cat said, handing him the key and the card. "The red one in the corner."

Even in the dark he had no trouble finding her. Her antennas stood very high up in front, aslant in the back, her crazy spotlights looked everywhere up at the sky and down at the ground, white and jet black was her top, and the red paint of her lowslung body was more than bright, luminous. Claude held the little card to the glow, reading it over. Then he stood off eyeing her a moment before he opened her trunk.

"O.K., pal?" the Cat called from the shack.

"I'll take her."

The battery might have started her had there been enough gas, but the Cat had five or six of the boys roll her over to the pump for a couple of gallons, a little shove with the pickup. Now she started off like thunder and lightning, and Claude stood up on the brakes to the end of the lot while the Cat walked beside holding the doors. The boys stood along the sidelines, cheering, and Claude reached under the dashboard to give them a blast with the wolf whistle. He braked her to a stop at the entrance, let her idle. "What sort of lady is this

Mrs. Merritt?'' he called, and the Cat cupped his ear.

"What?"

"What's with this Mrs. Merritt?"

Shoulders up, "I never saw her."

"Say, did anybody ever guess the price of that one?" he called, jabbing his finger at the roadster.

"What? Oh no, not yet," the Cat answered. "Guy by the name of Harry Halfenback came close, but we never did find him."

"You say he only came close?"

"What?"

"How close?"

"Oh, within a few shillings," mumbled the Cat. "I don't remember the details."

"Would he have won it?"

"What?"

"Would you have given it to him?"

"I don't get you."

"Would you let a man have it?"

"Hell, yes," the Cat said. "If we could find him."

Waving, Claude released brakes and eased the beast out on the street to a paternal thump on the fender and a gay "Take it easy!" He could see all the waving boys, their smiles somewhat magnified in his looking glasses, but he did not have time to give them the whistle. Ahead an old man hopped back up on the curb and stood lightly there on one foot waiting, smiling and nodding at Claude; his plump plaid bowling ball bag affording him balance. Claude did not stop for him. He gave the beast her head and she went for a caution light, loudly making it. All the leftover leaners were noticing him now, he could see them already turning to look in the block up ahead, looking in the block he was passing, and, in his magnifying glasses, several blocks back. At the next corner he came to with no stopsign or signal he headed her north. Oh, she could take corners. Climbing the steep hill past the office he had to contain her, she muttering angrily. Going down under rein she almost exploded. Two blocks from the room he pulled her off the road at a standard corner, bringing the pink-faced monkeys out of their glass house in a hurry. They pranced before her, coaxing her onto the rack. Claude remained inside for a while, until he was sure she was resting, then hopped out beside them. "Go over her carefully," he told them. "She's had a hard life."

"We get you."

At the room he shaved, showered, and thought to ask Emily Dix someday which way the paper should roll, toward the stool or the wall. Then he threw his things in his suitcase, not forgetting his tie. From the window sill he took the hard-boiled eggs he had prepared for his breakfasts, dumped them in the paper sack with the powdered coffee, and put in the salt shaker. The green bread he left for the cockroaches. It was that easy. His magnificent beast was already waiting for him at the fence when he got to the corner, the monkeys back in their house staring out at her. Placing his suitcase in her trunk, he hoped she would not think he was being too familiar. His eggs, coffee and salt he put in the glove-and-goggle compartment.

"Well, how was she?"

"Thirsty."

Oh, she was a gay one all right, but he picked up the tab without protest. For change the monkeys gave him a certain amount of respect, mixed with envy, and at his return she too eyed him from all angles, almost admiringly. She had found herself a good boy. As for himself, he was beginning to succumb to her power. Backing her out he let her breathe a little as they headed east on the darkest streets he could find, preferring to arouse the innocent populace than the police. His plan was to take her a few miles out of town, then pull over to the side of the road for some sleep. That way they would get a good headstart in the morning.

Two

He awoke on the desert gliding at seventyfive, to see
a single great headlight topping a rise not far off and
bearing toward him. Vaguely he remembered being under
the eye of the law most of the night, pursued by cops
in white cars like their uniforms, so he slowed her to an
unreasonable speed and crept on with two restless wheels
in the sand. Ahead of him the light veered off to the
right, out of disappointment or what, and it appeared
to rise quickly into the air. He soon saw why: it was
the moon being chased by the sun. He decided to stop
for some rest. Among other things the gas tank was
almost empty, or so read, and he would have to replenish
his strength and his humility before he would be ready
to walk. All this he tried to explain to her as gently as
he could with his foot. She was eager to keep on to the
end of the world, but she was beginning to show him a
little consideration which he hoped in time might grow
into love. Her lap was a firm one with a charming hint
of surrender.

He opened his eyes to find that the day was full grown
and the moon, desperately pale as with shock, had somehow eluded the sun. As it turned out Claude too had
cause to be thankful, for just over that next rise a little
brown town lay sprawled on its back. He guessed this
to be where the sun had his headquarters, at least spent
most of his time, so they approached at a cowardly pace
glancing aside at the billboards they passed. But he was
behind neither of them, no doubt he spent his afternoons
patrolling the roads. At the corner they stopped for a
few gallons of gas, a few quarts of oil. Claude decided
to leave her there and walk back to the store, for he

was beginning to learn that it was going to cost him more to keep her happy in the country than it would have in town. Besides he preferred that she not watch while he ate, as he too had a formidable appetite. He stood back in a corner furtively putting on fat, washing down big apples and donuts with half-and-half. It would be enough that she should see him nibbling eggs.

While he was in the store he bought two postcards, one of which he sent to the Bank of the Angels requesting them to transfer his savings to Arizona. He had no idea whether they would do such a thing, but he need not worry meanwhile, he had his savings bonds for defense. On the other card he had planned to send hello to an old friend named Sissy Lee, but he could not think of her address, although he remembered her in various other ways well. He believed Sissy would forgive him his single-mindedness; in any case the Miss looked too stately in front of her name. He bought a card with a picture of a Papago girl cradling a lamb in her arms and sent it to Anna Bloutz, whose address he would never forget. "Dear Ann, I decided to look for a new home. I like it out here. Write me in care of my sister at the address below if you are still there." In truth he had no idea where he was himself. The sign over the store read Arivada, which sounded familiar enough although he did not remember it as one of the new ones, far less the original.

Whether or not, he felt very much at home in this state. It was to places like this that they had sent him all over the world in defense of New York, until he had come almost to believe that the concrete caverns and towers he seemed dimly to remember, the pale people themselves, were no more than childhood fantasies he had dreamed for himself. He had felt little urge to try to find them again. Hopefully he had followed the Cat out to the new coast, only to find there the same grotesque imaginary cities already erected and fanatically maintained by old children. It was his loss alone that he could not play at their game with them, but he could not. He had been born in New York, taught the rules in New York and New England, yet it seemed to him that he had been holding his breath until he reached Arivada, New Africa. Here the dream cities, no matter whether adobe or gold, had long ago been abandoned, thus had collapsed, and all that remained was the earth. It spread around him as drab and coarse as an old army blanket, inviting only those weary with fighting or dying, overlooked by the children. If still in one piece the whole world would look like this in old age— Arivada was ready, but could Manhattan support mesquite?

Certainly nowhere but Arivada could support a man such as stood near the road a few miles ahead. Even at this distance out he had an air of belonging just where he was, like a great blue-skinned cactus that had stood there rooted in the sand and absorbing the sun long before anyone thought of making a road; in fact the road jogged a little where he was, as though they had detoured around him. But at closer view there was no room for doubting that this was a man. Packed solidly from his waist to his calves in pants intended for a plump little six-footer, he seemed to stand aloof from his crude ankle boots that even for him were outsized. He had a new blue shirt to go with his jeans, but had found no hat that would do. Nor did he carry anything but great handfuls of air at his sides. Claude could imagine the tourists passing him by, looking him over but no more thinking of stopping for him than for a giant saguaro to take home to the garden. Claude did stop, having seen him in plenty of time to put on the brakes. The man's head filled the window. "I am Pete," he said. "I will be in Pascua when it is light if you take me."

"I'm Claude," Claude said, "and get in." He reached for the door handle, but Pete knew about cars. He opened the door for himself, and when he was in he closed it and locked it. He held a big hand out to Claude. "I'm Pete," he repeated.

"I'm Claude," Claude said, shaking the hand. "Have you been standing there long?"

Pete looked at the side of the road, where a ring of wooden matches and cigarette papers lay mashed in the sand, while Claude started the car. "Only since morning," Pete said, but he did not mention which one. "Will you be in Pascua when it's light, mister?"

"I hope so."

Pete offered tobacco and paper, but Claude brought out his cigarettes and they both decided to try those. Pete provided the match. When he had thier cigarettes burning strongly he turned to look back at the road, then straight up ahead. "We'll get there for supper if we get there," he said, and Claude laughed. Pete was a young man, but had a wild old grin stretched all out of shape in the corners and punched full of holes. "I come from Wassonvee two mornings ago," he said, quickly sobering. "That's pretty fast time."

"Yes, it is."

"You come from Wassonvee too?"

"Wassonvee?"

"Wass-on-vee, Wass-on-vee—out by San Francisco."

"Oh no, I come from Los Angeles."

"Yes, I know that town," Pete said. "When did you come from there, since lunch?"

"Since last night," Claude said, smiling, but this time Pete kept himself grimly decorous. "I slept on the way."

Nodding, Pete put out his cigarette carefully in the ash tray and slipped it into his shirt pocket that didn't hold his tobacco and papers, buttoned the pocket. "You go to Pascua to the Ceremony?"

"No, I'm going to see someone there."

"I go to Pascua to be in the Ceremony," Pete said. "It's my vow. They took care of me five years ago when I got a fever in the river down there. They make me well, so since then I vow to come back each year to be in the Ceremony. This will be my last year though. Maybe I make my vow again this time, I'll see. You go to the Ceremony?''

"I'm going to visit someone this time." Claude said, "but I saw part of the Ceremony a few years ago when I was in the army."

"Maybe you saw me in there then?"

"I think maybe I did."

"I am wearing a mask, but I think maybe you saw me."

"Yes."

They were silent while Pete made himself a fresh cigarette. He offered Claude the tobacco, but Claude showed him how busy he was with the car. "You go to Pascua to see your mother?" Pete asked.

"No, my mother is in Boston."

"Bosson," Pete said. "My mother is dead in the ground in Sonora since six years ago. My father is there since almost twenty-more years ago. He couldn't live any more when they took the land away. What am I saying, he died of a breaking apart?"

"He died of a broken heart?"

"He died of a breaking heart," Pete said, making a stout log fence of his hands around the glove compartment and leaning forward to peer at the luminous clock, "but he was an old man. He was the king of his Yaquis down there and he couldn't live any more when they took the land away. He couldn't live up in the mountains that way. He hid all the treasures—you understand treasures?—in the mountains down there and he died. Now I'm the king of my Yaquis and someday I'll go down there and dig up the treasures again—maybe soon if they don't catch me too much. Then I buy the land back and we will live in the future like in the past only better." Pete let the fence fall, and sunlight showed the clock to be hours wrong, if not years.

"Do you know where this treasure is hidden?"

Pete took out his watch. "I know where it is if I can find it," he said, adjusting the time with a big thumb and forefinger. "I can find it. My father gave me a paper for that. That's why I save up my dollars, to go down there and find it. I put my dollars in the bank," he added, glancing at Claude. He slipped his watch in his pocket and leaned forward to stroke the face of the clock, erasing the fingerprints on it. "Soon I have enough money for my counter and my pick and my shovels and my food for three weeks enough for myself and another man or two men. That's why I work for the peaches in Wassonvee, to do that."

"Ah, you work in the peach orchards in Watsonville?"

"Sure," Pete said, "that's why I go back there after the Ceremony if they don't catch me. Soon maybe I have enough dollars to go down there. I'll see, maybe next year, maybe two years if they don't catch me too much."

"If who doesn't catch you?" asked Claude, offering Pete a cigarette which he accepted.

"Who?"

"Who wants to catch you?"

"Who, the patrol," Pete said. "They already catch me about twenty-more times and take me back down there, but I always come back. I don't have any paper for that. I used to have a patrone about a few years ago, but he gave me back to the patrol when I did all his work. He was no patrone. They took me back down there again after that, but I always know where to swim back in the night. They always want me to work for the peaches, sometimes for the apples and the arti-chokes and the lettuce. Sometimes I work for the yards and the swimming pools, I don't care. You don't work for the patrol."

"No no."

"You don't work for the patrol in this car," Pete told him.

She must have heard him, or they were closely attuned,

for seconds later she blew a rear tire. It went off as quietly as a rifle, and Claude might not even have noticed but for Pete tipping toward him and leaning uphill to the ashtray. She held as straight to her course as a bull, plainly ready to continue on as though nothing had happened. Nevertheless she responded to Claude's foot more quickly than usual. When she was grounded they glanced briefly at one another, then they got out.

"That's not much tire there," Pete said.

"I should have noticed it sooner," Claude said, unlocking the trunk. "I hope this damned jack works."

"It works all right," Pete said, taking the jack from Claude's hand. He had the beast high in the air in less time than it took Claude to pull off her skirt, and he gave the jack a stiff kick as if letting it know that should it decide to fall down he could hold the beast up himself. Not until Claude handed him the lug-wrench did he pause in his work. Squatting beside the wheel he turned it upside down, but it came to a point at that end. He pounded with a rock until it hung unassisted from one of the lugs, but it was simply too small to take hold. Claude tried for a while, giving up as soon as he got it to hang there. It fell off and Pete tossed it aside. "Do you have a pliers?"

"I doubt that," Claude said, but marvelously there was a pair in the glove-and-goggle compartment.

"Do you have a cloth?" Pete seemed to know that he was asking too much. He brought out his new handkerchief, wrapped it around the handles of the pliers before he leaned over the wheel. He went up on the square toes of his boots. His hands swelled to twice their extraordinary size as he pressed down on a lug, his neck too expanding, a band of molten copper overflowing the black line of his hair, the blue line of his shirt. Claude stepped back, giving Pete room, waiting for something to break. Pete grunted, and the pliers gave way a little under his hands. He grunted again and they fell to the ground. His trembling fingers quickly twirled off the nut and flipped it over to the hubcap, where it stayed. He went in that way from one lug to the next around the wheel, Claude quietly cheering him each time the pliers fell. The last was the hardest of all. Either it was welded there, or Pete was losing some of his strength. He was losing some of his patience. He took up his rock in both hands and pounded mightily on the lug until it sheared. "You don't need that one," he said, tossing it over his head and slipping the wheel off. He stood up wiping his shiny copperplate face.

"I didn't think you could do it," Claude said.

"Who?"

"I didn't think anyone could do it with pliers."

Rolling the spare wheel into place, Pete kicked the pliers aside. "That pliers is too light." He lifted the wheel easily with one hand, held it in place briefly before letting it down. Now he lifted it once more, this time holding it there. It was as though he still had his strength, but had lost all will to finish the job; he could hold the wheel up forever, but he could not put it on. Claude finally took it from his hands and let it fall to the ground. Pete squatted beside the wheel wiping his face gently, high up on his sleeve. Then he reached down to finger the tread and bounce his knuckles on the while wall of the tire: the rubber was firm. He flipped the wheel backside up. It had lately been painted, over the original green, a brilliant red not unlike the red of the four other wheels. It seemed to be the right kind, had five, the proper number of holes, all the same size, only each hole was a quarter of an inch too far from the next hole to fit over the lugs. "Where did you get a car like this one?"

"From my father," Claude said, and Pete opened his eyes. At first Pete's face cracked only a little, almost imperceptibly, along certain weak lines, but as he looked from Claude to Claude's spare to Claude's car back to Claude his whole head broke apart in that wild lurid grin, and his body was shaking somewhere inside. His belly was shaking, and he bent low over his folding arms, bouncing a little, trying to soothe it. Whenever it seemed that he had himself under control he would reach out to rap weakly that impeccable tire, topple helplessly forward hugging his pain on the ground. Claude tried not to look at Pete, but not as hard as he tried to see him, for he too found himself falling apart. Now they both were on the ground, writhing, looking at one another when they were able, in moments of quiet half-lifting themselves to slap that tire, fall back roaring or silently crying, so that it seemed they would go on forever. Yet they did stop at last, too soon, sadly. They were stretched on their backs gasping for air when the highway scrapers came upon them from behind.

"What seems to be the trouble down there?"

They got to their feet explaining as well as they could, pointing and kicking, describing, the car, the wrench, the pliers, that tire. The highway workers too found it rather amusing, and they shook their heads as they loaded the blowout and the spare onto their scraper. Luckily for the travelers there was a Mexaco station not many miles down the road, open for business under new management twentyfour hours a day. The new owner listened to their story with interest; he believed he could take care of them. He could not trade them a Thunderhead wheel for their spare, but he thought he had a good one in back he could sell them. Claude told him that he did not believe Mrs. Merritt would accept a bill of more than ten dollars, so that was what he charged, and he himself picked them out a nice tire that had plenty of miles on it. He even threw in a big lug wrench for their small one. As for the highwaymen, they could not accept payment for their trouble, but they had never been known to turn down a little beer money. They liked cigarettes too. Taking the travelers back to their car, they gaily went over the story again, with its happy ending, and among them they got that new tire on almost as quickly as Pete could have alone. He wouldn't get that one off with pliers, for damn sure. When they had finally passed on, the travelers delayed their journey long enough to wipe the grease and red paint off their hands with Pete's handkerchief and fire up Claude's last cigarettes. "Hey, you've got a nice car now," Pete said, closing and locking his door.

Starting the beast Claude asked Pete not to tempt her, for a minute. Pete did better than that, he remained for five minutes stoically smoking, and then he raised his hands in the air before speaking. "Stop right here," he said. "I like to take a present to my friends in Pascua."

"Here? A present?" Claude asked, braking the beast.

Pete did not immediately answer, but climbed out of the car, and Claude followed. He had to move fast to keep up with Pete on the desert. "It must be a hot spring here," Pete said. "These flowers are early."

"What flowers?"

"It must be a very hot spring here," Pete said.

"It seems cool to me."

"Sure, that's why the flowers are showing in daytime."

"What flowers!"

For answer Pete picked up a stone and threw it thirty feet in the air at a nearby saguaro; when the stone dropped from the top, something dropped with it. Pete collected a handful of stones and threw them rapidly in series. Every time, almost every time he threw one, a flower sailed down. Each had its own cornucopia attached, green and fleshy, elongated, like a small artichoke squeezed out of shape by large hands. Most of the flowers were closed, but a few had their white waxen petals distended generously in handfuls. They were beginning to pile up on the ground. Claude selected a good rock and let fly. It must have been a very hot spring here, if Pete said so. Claude looked back at the road, saw that there were two cars parked there now. The one in the rear also had tall antennas, and a cop was out and walking around the beast carefully. His white uniform, sunburned and sandblasted, needed laundering. Now he interrupted his tour to look out at the desert. Claude looked around too, but he was alone there, he and the saguaros. He walked back to the road, hands at sides, clearly visible, bearing humility. No man in his right mind approaches a cop without such an offering.

"Are you the owner of this car?" A cop has something you don't have, something you gave him earlier.

"No, I'm just delivering it to Oklahoma City for a lady."

"Do you have plates for this car?" A cop needn't be vicious, but he can be so, safely.

"Just those stickers."

"Do you have the registration?" Presidents and premiers can annihilate millions, but only a cop can explain away your solitary murder.

"Well, I have this card here."

The officer took the card carefully with his left hand, then lowered his eyes to it. He can be far psycho—and lock you up, forevermore. "Are you Claude Squires?"

"Yes, I am."

"Is this your signature here?"

"No, that's my father's. He owns the A-I Drive-away Agency, and I'm delivering this car to Mrs. Merritt in Oklahoma City for him."

"How did he get possession of this car?"

"I don't know. I suppose Mrs. Merritt left it with him."

"Who's this Mrs. Merritt?"

Shrugging Claude said, "I never saw her."

The officer continued his tour of the car. He pried at the hood with his fingers, and Claude reached through the window to release it for him. After raising the hood, the officer went back to his own car for a flashlight, returning selected a sharp rock from the roadbed. Now he leaned over the fender to scrape slime from the motor, compare the number there with the one on the card. For the minute or two the cop remained there folded, up on tiptoe, with rock and flashlight clanking inside, Claude felt his own life hang in the cop's tense awkward balance. Any but the most discreet, toward gesture, any unplanned move or sound, a sneeze, itch, a gnat in the ear, would have been enough to finish him. He even knew the precise spot in his belly where he would be blasted; it shivered. Claude made no move to soothe it. Pivoting slowly the perfect murderer said, "Those numbers don't coincide."

"Don't they, officer?" Moving gently, tenderly accepting the flashlight, Claude too checked them. They were identical till near the end, but concluded 578 on the motor, 578 on the card. Softly, "That must be an error in copying."

"On the engine or the card?"

"On the card."

The officer looked again, shaking his head. "That's a big discrepancy for a engine number," he said, fingering the wolf whistle. He straightened his back and looked out at the desert. "What were you doing out there anyway?"

"Gathering flowers."

The officer walked around the beast and out on the desert with Claude, a halfstep behind Claude. When they reached the saguaro he looked around at the ground, up in the air, down at the ground again. "What did you say your name was?"

"Claude Squires."

"How did you get those flowers, Carl?" the officer asked.

"I threw stones at them," Claude told him.

Together the officer and Claude looked up at the saguaro.

[64]

"What are you, a ball player?"

"No no."

The officer picked up a rock, but he did not throw it. He bounced it on his palm a few times before he dropped it among the flowers. "I think you better come back to the office with me, Carl," he said as they walked, as though side by side, to the road.

The officer slammed the beast's hood down. Claude, while the officer maneuvered to his own car, looked once more at the desert. For almost as far as he could see, the saguaros had it all to themselves. Huge and decrepit with age, their bodies bearing uncountable pale scars, welts, black bruises, riddled with holes, their cumbersome arms, when they had any, held straight up in the air by little more than indomitable habit, they stood their ground alone, haughty, magnificent, not giving a damn for this hell they were guarding alone and forever. The ocotillo and mesquite strung thinly at their feet was no more than a token resistance. The rocks themselves were mean ones, almost all of a size to be thrown easily by a strong man, none to hide him. The officer swung his car in front of the beast, prepared to show Claude where the town was.

They stopped before a building the size and shape of a barbershop, similarly windowed, and Claude walked forward to the patrol car in time to hear the radio barking. "Call that drive-away agency, if they can't straighten out that discrepancy then hold him until he finds someone who can," and an enthusiastic "10-4" from the officer hopping out of his car. They walked cop-foremost into the office, where one considerable man sat astir at his desk. He had nothing to say to them, for he had just said it all on the air. But now the officer did two things at once, picked up the phone and reread Claude's card. "What did you say your name was again?" It was still Claude, he seemed disappointed. He shoved the phone at Claude, ran into the back room.

"Collect," growled the man at the desk.

The clock on the wall claimed twenty past five. While the girls, loathe to permit him to talk to himself person to person, even collect, were trying to fathom the complex relationship of father and son, Claude had time to ask himself where the Cat might be at this indifferent hour, whether at the clubhouse drinking his milk, or out on the prowl. He was fearful, and his voice fell when he heard who answered the phone. "This is Claude," he interrupted the girls. "Is the Cat there?" "Youbetcha," Harry Halfenback said, for he was a good, good boy who knew all the right words. The Cat accepting the call, Claude explained to him as quickly as he could the discrepancy, the S and the 5, the evidence pointing to an error in copying.

The Cat, a good listener over the phone, had only one thing to ask: "Where the hell are you?"

"Some little town in Arivada, I think."

"Well, hold on a minute," the Cat said. It took him half that time to return from the shack. "Let me see now," he said, to a rattling of papers and a clinking of cups. "Yes, it's an error in copying all right. The correct reading is 5 . . ."

"Just a minute—this is Sergeant Lord. You say it's all right, sir?" Claude could hear the sergeant's voice equally well with both ears—both ways unhappy. "That's a big discrepancy for a engine number, sir. We want to be sure."

"Yes, I have the papers here before me on my desk, sergeant," said the Cat. "Now will you please deliver that car to Mrs. Merritt as quickly as possible, Claude."

"O.K., and thanks."

"Thanks for your trouble, sir."

"No trouble."

They all dropped their phones, and Claude waited for the cop to return from the back room. The cop handed Claude his discrepant release without comment. "Well, I guess it was just an error in copying," Claude said, and when no one agreed: "Well, I guess I'd better be on my way if I hope to get to Arizona by suppertime."

"You're in Arizona," muttered the one, and the other was typing amok. Cops are here to protect us.

Nobody accompanied Claude to the door, but by the time he had the beast started the patrol car was pulling away from the curb. Claude followed as far as the corner, turned in for a refuel, permitting the cop to get a good headstart to the east. Unfortunately there were no complete blocks in this town, to circle, but heading west past the office he was able to keep the beast almost quiet, and he did not let himself glance inside to see whether the big man was clerking or radio talking. Once out of sight of the town, he let the beast do it her way, thus it was not long before they spotted Pete big and blue up ahead by the side of the road. They had surprised him with his arms down, but now he raised them up high. He was leaning forward a little, the ground at his feet was well tamped, and there were other small signs of transplanting. He was perspiring. When they stopped beside him he put his head in the window. "Hey, did they catch you?"

"Yes, and where the hell did you disappear to?"

"Out there," Pete said, waving toward the desert. "When I see them catch you I think maybe I have to find a new car to drive me. I think maybe they send you back to Los Angeles."

"Not yet," Claude said, "but you'd better get in the back seat and lie low if you want to get to Pascua this year."

Pete knew about cars. He climbed in and lay at once on his back, not folded but packed there, peacefully smoking. "What's the matter," he asked, as Claude turned the beast around, "they didn't like you and your car?"

"Not very much. They thought I had stolen her."

"You showed them your papers?"

"Yes, but my papers don't have the same number as my car."

"Number! You mean they make more cars like this one?"

"Pete, you'd better lie quiet until we get through Arivada."

Pete obeyed, but a moment later Claude felt a tap on his shoulder; glancing in the mirror, he reached back for the cigarette Pete had made him. Firing it up, he found it to be just what he needed. Not only did it have a fine aroma and flavor, it gave him a new sense of belonging. He slowed the beast well in advance of the limits, but even so she farted once in front of the office. Claude, holding his breath, did his best to ignore her. They got through town just in time. The cop, tired of waiting out east, was prowling back in, radio talking. Claude shook his head as they passed: oh this beast was a thirsty one. He drove the next twenty miles at the limit plus three, his eyes fixed on her looking glasses, before he gave Pete the all clear.

"Did we make it?" Pete eased himself onto the front seat.

"I think so."

Pete undid the top botton of his shirt, revealing to Claude a binful of perverted artichokes with their white flowers primly compressed.

"I thought you looked a little fuller than usual."

"These will make a nice present for my friends in Pascua," Pete said. "Tonight we will cool them with water inside and tomorrow they will show themselves nicely. Then the others will throw them at me three times and soon I will be won over to His side. The flowers will win me. Flowers have the force of good, they chase away evil."

"It's a good thing we stopped for them."

"I don't think we will be there for supper though."

Claude drew the paper sack from the glove-and-goggle

compartment, and now for awhile they drove on too absorbed, too hungrily absorbing, for either silence or talking, Pete doing the cracking and peeling and salting. When they had finished, Pete took out his tobacco and rolled one for Claude. "We get there pretty quick now," he said, firing it for him.

"Yes."

"You go to see someone in Pascua?"

"Yes, a girl."

"You want this girl for your marry?"

"My marry? No, I don't know her that well. I met her just before I got out of the army."

"She is pretty?"

"She's all right. Not very."

"You like her?"

"I think so."

"Some time when I buy my land back I will find a nice girl that I like to have for my marry and we will live on the land with a big family. But I don't have a chance for that these days. I'll see about that after I find my treasure."

"How much money will you need to go find it?"

Pete considered a minute. "I think maybe a thousand dollars, maybe if they catch me too much only six hundred dollars. I'll see how long it takes me. That's why I don't have a chance for the girls now. It's too much running and swimming. . . . Hey, there she is now!" he said, for as they broke over a rise she suddenly blossomed in the cool air they were entering, her brightness making them aware for the first time of their own darkness, her luminous road signs seeking to reassure them, they would soon be in Tucson. Pete buttoned his shirt. "We didn't get there when it was light," he said, "but we had a good supper."

"Oh yes."

"She is fatter than last year."

"She's much fatter than four years ago." They were

already inside her.

"I think someday she will get too fat and swallow up the desert."

Claude said, "Maybe."

"Hey, your girl is waiting for you down there," Pete said, smoothing his hair, "and my friends in Pascua are waiting for me."

"Sure."

They glided past the glowing motels, Pete exclaiming, Claude driving, agreeing, and Pete had his door unlocked and half-open by the time they stopped at the block-square village of Pascua not far from the center of town. "Hey, we made it."

Claude smiled. "Well, when I make my first thousand dollars I'll look you up and we'll go find that treasure."

"Hey, me too," Pete said. "We could find it together."

"Good luck to you, Pete."

"Good luck to you, mister." They shook hands through the window, and Pete turned toward Pascua. Someone was already waving.

Claude continued on to the dead center of town, noting another bookstore gone, the Gaiety Theater closed, beside a glassy-eyed new First Trust, turned right on the wide street leading to the south side where the motels glowed more modestly and a few proud old street-lamps glared sadly at the dark, glaucoma setting in. Now he crept along carefully observing, until he discovered a little sign blinking bluely between a grocery and an osteopath, parked the beast a half-block beyond lest MRS WHITES might think he wished to hold up her MOTEL*MOTEL*MOTEL, or buy it. Even so she greeted his entrance with white-faced supplication, she was old, had nothing, until he brought out his wallet; then she set to work at once, while she sought her guest-book, her inkwell and her glasses, singing, droning, paralyzing him to mindless rest, there would be a bed, there would be fresh desert air, there would be quiet, there would be high old spirits such as he had not tasted for many a night. He paid her the three dollars before he hiked back for the beast.

His cabin, the fifth of five, reminded him of home, except that here was a tiny private shower, a tiny electric icebox, and on the chair a self-conscious telephone. It was in this the order of their importance that he used, or thought to use them, finding the water warm, the icetray too, the phone, even had there been a directory, much too handy to suit his mood. What to say, hello, remember me, I just got in, I'm here? It seemed he had a headache, rare for him, or perhaps he had no head at all. He looked with sudden dejection around this hole he had come so far and earnestly to cower in. Perhaps next door for beer, but then sit up all night waiting for that box to cool? Or rest a while? Sleep had never solved much for him. He got up from the bed to stare at himself in the crazy mirror, but turned away, he hated fools. Since he was here, the least compromising thing for him to do was ask Information-O for the number, only, and then head slowly, pensively, back uptown. It delighted him to find that the phone was dead.

With such luck as this, he rode the beast in the jaunty way that she deserved, back north, seemingly back from Mexico, pulling up finally at an outlying bar-ex-saloon (they had covered the old adobe face with knotty pine, substituted big stone matades for the cuspidors) and having brought her wrecklessly this far did not park her in the little parking lot but in front of the church next door. They had lifted that face too and neonized, but it did no good, they seemed to know they had no chance against an older god, their doors were closed. Thus one could join the pagan worshipers with a self-righteous shrug, through latticed doors. There weren't many here, two in cowboy hats to shade their blood-red eyes, and long-heeled boots to hang their skinny legs on stools, two in yet-damp working clothes, one in polite shirt and pants who eyed the only girl like a four-balled Kirk McBrando Barrymore. Claude could let himself expand in such company: not one of these had just traversed Arivada in a Thunderhead, not one had a little girl in town who wrote by airmail that she wished to go to bed with him, thus not one had precious time to kill. Seated beside the white-collared lech he ordered a boilermaker, not wishing to be rushed into anything he wasn't ready for, and searing and smoothing his throat by turns he believed that waiting thus four years ago he also would have played for that not-so-distant girl (he seemed to be getting through to her better anyhow) out of youthful extravagance. Tonight he cooled off with a second beer, maturely considering his annoying predicament. He began a third: still he could think of nothing better to do than telephone.

This phone was a live one, the operator too, and a voice was home. "Vivien?"

"Yes."

"This is Bill."

"Bill who?"

"Viv, what are you doing tonight?"

"Bill who?"

"You know, *Bill*, down at the office the other day. What are you doing tonight?"

"Making dinner. Goodbye," she said.

"Hey wait—it's Bill, Bill, a friend of Whatsername . . . "

"I don't know her either," she said, "goodbye."

It seemed she didn't make friends easily. He called again. "Viv?"

"Is it you again?"

"No—Claude. Claude Squires."

"Claude Squires," she said.

He waited some time for her to add to that, but "Vivien? Are you there?" at last.

"Yes, where are *you*?"

"Oh, I'm down south."

"How *far* down south?"

"I don't know, a mile or two."

"You're here in town!"

"Yes, I got in a while ago . . . "

"Claude, where did you come from?"

"West."

"Then you got my letter?"

"Yes, I got it the other day." Yesterday.

"Then . . . "

"I'm passing through, as the saying goes," he interrupted her. "I have this car . . . "

"Ah, I see."

"Well, you talk too fast when you talk," he said.

"I know. I'm sorry," and he heard she was. "Where shall I meet you, Claude?"

"I'll call for you."

"No, let me meet you, Claude!"

"We tried that once four years ago." He laughed alone.

"Claude, please. Everyone's here . . . "

"Good, I'll rescue you."

Her "Please" was a wail this time.

"I'll be right out, Viv," he told her. "Stop making dinner and put on your shoes."

"You don't even know where I live . . . "

"I'll look in the directory," and hanging up he returned to the bar for the rest of his beer before he went out to hunt for a telephone. That lone girl was gone.

The booth he chose was in a drugstore adjoining the railroad station, in the Hotel El Mirage, where he had first, and last, met Eleanor. He had been rising from the counter, orange juice, just as she, every flawless bit of her, had been slipping in, and her impetuous level look had decided that they were both world travelers (he had been wearing his civil weekend suit) in an unheard-of town, they both would have to spend the night somewhere here, they both looked clean, she already had a room. . . . So he had sat down again. She was a lively lady making some man a lively and expensive wife, but he had found no time to ask her who, she knowing so many exotic languages, speaking them so well. Tonight she probably would not have noticed him, in his shirt sleeves and sharp-toed shoes, had she been there. He probably would have done no more than notice her. In four years he had lost most of his military overbearing, not to mention some of his curiosity.

As for Vivien (he remembered that he had her letter in his pocket still) it turned out that she lived by chance in a residential neighborhood, northeast of town. He had guessed as much. What surprised him was his sudden eagerness to be out there. Perhaps he had changed more in four years than was good for him. Not even the sight of her tightly curbed and gutterless slice of town, reduced to naught by a realtor's simple arithmetic, could quite dishearten him, nor even her stillborn house laid out in sad new finery with all the rest. He parked the beast squarely in front of her house, and with a firm step walked that walk leading as straight as a plank to her front door, a real buccaneer. And he didn't even have to press the bell or strike the gong to walk, without breaking stride, into her arms. She did not actually embrace him, but the sense of it was there as she stood as though barring all the world from some private memory of him, which his silly smile did everything in its power to depreciate. They hung thus for at least a minute before she thought to step back and say "Come in."

He did, and now it was his memory of her she brought up short in the candid light of the fluorescent hall, for her plainness became all at once a thing of depth only hinted at by the door-framed silhouette (it seemed he had remembered her so, in silhouette) and he had to read all over again the subtle language of her face with its dark, withdrawing eyes, her long russet hair that memory glossed, her slender, unpretentious body which she left free for the imagination to enhance, wherever necessary. In brief she was a sharp rebuff to the forgetful eye, and yet her voice invited another look. "I'm sorry I didn't recognize you on the telephone."

"What to expect? I'm out of uniform."

"Still, you haven't changed."

"Neither have you," he said.

"Yes, I have," Vivien said, and she seemed ready to explain to him exactly how she had, when a voice somewhere inside called a hearty "Come on in," and turning to look for the source of her sudden unhappiness he felt her warm breath against his ear, heard her whisper, "Just long enough to say hello."

The invitation had come from the man who sat in a chair with his back to them, but Vivien led Claude to the far end of the room where an old lady sat facing the door and yet took no notice of their approach. Only when Vivien darted forward to brush her arm did she look up with slow-motion eyes and then she brought, it seemed reluctantly, her lower jaw up too. She watched Vivien's silent lips explain something to her at length, or rather repeat a word, his name, again and again, before she moved her eyes to look at him. Now she waited for him to say, aloud, "Hello, Mrs. James," before she held up her limp hand and faintly smiled. "Hello," her lips said, and her jaw fell down.

That was all there was. Vivien took Claude's hand and they turned away, walked stiff-armed together to the other end of the room. The man there waited until they had reached his chair before he rose to his feet, languidly. He smiled his recognition of them both, but for Claude there was nothing memorable in his large soft face, his sloping shoulder line, his lax hands which he held one over the other at his crotch. Claude might have been looking at him for the first time—but for the orange hair, which he had let grow long and loose like the rest of him. Its unnatural gaiety brought back to mind an otherwise drab young man, or boy, in navy beige, and at the same time, while they waited to be reintroduced, Claude noticed that Vivien was wearing a bright scarlet dress.

"Claude, you remember Paul."

"Yes."

"It was in my car," Paul said, holding out a soft hand and smile. He had orange gums. "Late one night?"

"That's right," and just in time you got there too, Lieutenant, thought Claude, smiling and pressing fat.

"I believe I had the Lincoln then."

"I think so, yes."

"Big old bastard, wasn't it?" Smiling, nodding affirmation to himself, Paul withdrew his hand and waved it toward a chair, a straight-backed one not far from his. "Sit down," he said.

Claude glancing at Vivien saw her face as cramped and urgent as the message, written on a scrap of paper on her lap and in the dark, which she had shoved into his hand that night while Paul was driving him to the bus stop. Probably her face had also looked like this a few minutes earlier on that same night, in the wide back seat of the car behind the USO, but Claude had been looking at Paul instead. He had only dimly been able to see Paul looking in at them beneath the stiff shadow of his braided cap, and now his uneasy memory of that look made him glance at Paul's face again. There was pale smiling rage in it. "Sit down," Paul said.

Claude, waving and smiling too, said "Thanks, but we'll have to be on our way if we hope to find a restaurant."

"No, you're eating here with us. Vivien is making our supper anyway, as she always does, so she'll just throw in another can or two. It will be plain, modest fare, I fear, but tenderly prepared and served. Won't it,

Vi?'' He glanced at Vivien and she stared back, neither yes nor no, and then her lips said something softly sibilant. For a moment it seemed Paul either had failed to catch the word or did not care. He'd heard, he cared. Smiling his gummy smile he said, ''Vi, hadn't you better trot in and check those pans?'' and waited smiling for her to go. He did not look after her, he watched Claude look. ''Sit down.''

Seated Claude watched Paul, observed his loose hand sweep up his drink for the ever-smiling lips to swill before he traded it for the other big glass standing ready there, splashed whiskey into this one from the half-gone fifth he had, stale soda from the uncorked bottle on the floor, held it out, part way, to Claude, no ice, no stir. But with a smile: if Claude was finicky, too too bad, he'd drink it anyway. ''Cheers.''

''Cheers,'' Claude said, drinking it.

Paul poured himself another one. A model host, he made his own with no more fuss or whiskey than he had his guest's. Now he sat back with his hands wrapped around the glass as though warming it, his legs stretched out uncrossed toward Claude. ''What're you doing with yourself these days, Claude?''

''Just now I'm traveling . . . ''

''For whom?''

''Just traveling.''

''Ah.'' Paul smiled, nodded, that was fun.

''And you?''

''Engineering,'' Paul said, adding coyly, ''Civ-il,'' but his smile was too limp to support irony. ''When did you get out?''

''Out?''

''Of the bird force, yes.''

''Right after you saw me, the next week or so.''

''Oh ho, you were one of the privileged ones.'' Paul drank to him. ''Me they sent out on another Pacific pleasure cruise as soon as my leave was up, on the U.S.S.

Washingmachine. Where is she now? In drydock at Norfolk, Virginia, I think. We were supposed to be gone two months, so it took us six. We spent almost half that time off the island of Layu, in the Phillapees. Let's see—August 1st to October 29th, just about three months. Nothing much was happening, but we were standing by in case something, insurrection, etc., did— there was still unrest, a few people were getting knocked off everyday, mostly civilians though. Naturally we had plenty of shore leave and plenty of time to kill— in fact four of we officers had a permanent lease on a penthouse atop the El Comode Hotel. There was plenty of good swimming, sousing, whoring whenever we wanted it. Have you noticed how whenever you drive very far in a car, get bored, you sooner or later have a hard one sitting there, or standing up—yah high—begging for attention after all that neglect?''

"Oh yes."

"Well, that's how it is after twentyeight days aboard ship. But Christ, black pussy walked the streets like vermin in those days on Layu, all you had to do was step out the hotel door with your fly unzipped. A pack of butts was the asking price, but a good chocolate bar would do. Some of the enlisted men weren't so happy though. Their hotels were over on the other side of town, near the native quarter, and since that section was off limits they had to rely on whatever came across the line. Most of the good stuff walked right on past them to hook up with we officers. What's more, a lot of those little brown gals preferred the nigra boys, and there were eightythree nigras on the U.S.S. Washingmachine. I remember one night when a couple of us were out prowling around, we heard this little yip and moan in an alley as we were passing, so we stopped for a look. We thought someone was beating a dog in there. Well, five sailors had this nigra boy down on the ground with his pants pulled down. One of them had a pocket knife

—yay big." He held a big pearl-handled knife in his hand and the long blade sprang out. "The others were holding the nigra's arms and legs while he performed a little operation on him. He had made his first exploratory incision—" Paul's blade sliced air— "but when he saw us standing there he stopped. The others too. (Hell, we weren't about to interfere, not with five of them.) You know that nigra boy didn't wait for his pants or anything, he took off past us like a damned kangaroo and ran down the street with his jumper flapping like a white flag over his black ass." Paul stopped to drink, laugh, shake his head while Claude stepped away to put his cigarette out in a glass candy dish. "You could see that one severed ball flapping halfway down to his knees, and he left a trail of blood as straight as a torpedo down the street. We didn't follow it, we . . . "

"Excuse me, Paul," Claude said from the diningroom door. "I'm going for ice . . . " She was at the stove, or standing near it, but he went directly to the box. They had fancy shallow icetrays with small plastic cups, some half-filled, that could be lifted out individually. He had plunked the ice from six of these into his glass when he heard her behind his back. Turning he looked down at her. "Shucks," he said.

"I know. I warned you, Claude."

"Let's get out of here."

"Not yet," she said, looking at her hand on his wrist she held. "It's safer to wait until he passes out."

"Safer?"

"Believe me, it'll be better. He'll be out cold by ten."

Glancing at the clock he shrugged. "What, are we afraid of him?" But he returned the plastic cups to their tray and quietly closed the door.

"I'll go back in with you." Untying her frilly apron she hung it, like a model little modern housewife, on a hook meant for it beside the door. Yet being led through the dining room by her was like being shown the short way to hell by a feverish crocodile. Paul was expecting them. Paul stood up smiling at their approach, waited until they were seated together on the couch before he sagged slowly into his chair.

"How's supper coming, Vi?"

"It won't be long."

"She means time for another highball," Paul said, sloshing one. "Claude? Ah, I see you're nursing yours. You were never in the navy, that's for sure. Vi, Claude here and I have been swapping war yarns. I was just telling him about that night on the isle of Layu when some of the men tried to castrate a nigra boy. I hadn't quite finished it, had I, Claude? Let's see. After that black boy bolted most of the sailors bolted too, but we stopped one and talked to him. He said they honestly intended to cut off his balls—excuse me, testicles. Some guy in the black market had promised them ten dollars a pair for them. It seems out there they like to eat the things, consider them a delicacy." Over his glass he shook his head at Claude. "I've never tried them myself, have you?"

"No, I haven't, Paul," Claude said, putting down his drink and leaning forward with his elbows resting on his knees, "but I remember a place where they could have picked up lots of them. Let's see. It was out on the desert of North Afucka, northwest of Dongola, I mean. Wait a minute, it was June 23rd of some damn year. This was my first junket overseas and I was what my c. o. called temporarily unattached, i.e. handyman. Naturally I had plenty of free time on my hands, plenty of sunbathing, sandpainting, and flies to kill whenever I wanted one. I remember the night very well, it was still light but the sun and the flies had gone and it was just turning cool—I had a fat case of gippy tummy and I was taking a little stroll, trying to work up an appetite. There was nothing unusual about the truck parked by itself a little beyond the camp, it was an ordinary open-bed truck, Dodge, similar to the old-fashioned garbage truck—it was the stink that attracted me. No garbage truck I'd ever seen had ever smelled like that. I think I knew at once what was causing it, but I walked over for a look anyway, or perhaps because. The driver must have been waiting in chowline with everyone else—I could see them lined up about half a mile away—so I was all alone. I remember how I stood up in back on my right foot, how the steel bumper felt, slippery, beneath the leather arch of my new shoe, and how I held onto the tailboard with both my hands. He had a full load of soldiers in his truck, thrown in, their arms and legs and heads in various positions and attitudes that I'd never seen before. They were mostly French, a few Arabs, and despite their uniforms they didn't look very important any more. Later I learned that if you watch men die, especially if you've known them at all, they still look important afterward no matter what you have to do with them, but I was inexperienced then. What I saw then was a little boy curled up in there on a soldier's chest, in a sort of nest of arms and legs. He looked comfortable, as though he were sleeping comfortably. He was near the back of the truck, so by putting both feet on the bumper and leaning over the tailboard I could reach out to him without touching much of anything else. I lifted him up and jumped backwards down to the ground, almost dropping him, but not. He was very light. I carried him quite a long way away before I laid him down on the sand. I didn't have any doubt about him by now, of course. He stank too. He looked about eight years old, but as I look at it now he was probably older than that and small for his age. He had on longish short pants, down to his knees, and a little short-sleeved khaki shirt, no shoes but you could see by the contrast between his pale ankles and skinny brown legs where they had been. Thank God his eyes were closed. Not having a shovel I looked around for something I could use to dig. There wasn't a damn thing anywhere for as far as I could see, not even a stick, so I came back to him. I suddenly felt guilty—very guilty about having brought him out there, squatting over him and looking at him, looking around me all the time to see if anyone was observing me. I picked him up again and carried him quickly back to the truck and dumped him in, not even looking after him. Then I started running—I remember wondering if I could have caught some disease from carrying him. I must have run about three or four hundred yards before I turned and ran back again. This time I had to walk on them to get him and bring him back. I curled him up on the soldier's chest again, in that little nest, trying very hard to arrange him exactly as he had been, but no matter what I did I couldn't make him look as comfortable as he had before. That's when I learned that death doesn't lie all under grass and every time I hear a war story I smell that stink again." He stopped, feeling now the heat of Vivien's thigh pressed against his as he bent forward to reach for his drink. He heard but didn't watch Paul swilling too.

"Speaking of stiffs," Paul said, his voice guttural, wet, "I remember one . . . "

"Paul, God damn you, why don't you shut up!"

Paul did shut up. For a moment his wide curving mouth was like something seen underwater, compressed, but undulating a little in the uncertain light, and his knife stood erect slowly in his lap like a secret claw about to strike. But now it sank as slowly down again, the lips fell apart, and he was smiling behind his drink, gurgling, "I didn't know you were squeamish, Vi. You didn't used to be." He reached for his bottle and held it for a moment tipped toward his glass, while he stared with her, but mockingly, at her hands clenched in her lap. "You didn't used to be."

"Paul, let's eat!"

"A fine idea." He stood up, gathering his glass, the

bottle, the knife all in one big hand but leaving the almost empty soda bottle on the floor, preceded them into the diningroom. Claude waited while Vivien went after Mrs. James, he stood in the doorway watching how she steered the chair carefully between the table legs, pushing it far in, until the old lady's chin hung above her silverware. It seemed she could feed herself. At Paul's invitation Claude sat down. Paul was already seated opposite Mrs. James, with his bottle and glass before him, his knife off to his right between his hand and Claude's, Claude's left, and a few inches closer to his own. They watched in silence Vivien bringing in the food and serving it, first Mrs. James's, next Claude's by way of Paul, then Paul's which he also passed on to Claude. Claude placed the dish beside Paul's knife. Paul grinned. "Claude here and I have had a chance to get to know one another better," he said, moving the dish to his other side. "Claude was one of the privileged ones. He got out of the bird force soon after we met him that night. That's why we never saw him again."

"Is it," Vivien said.

"Yes, Claude didn't waste any more time than he had to in Arizona, he took off from here the same day they let him out, eh, Claude? Claude was bored. He wanted to go out to Hollywood and mix with the movie stars. Oh, he's had a gay life these past few years, you can tell that all right. Claude, is it true what they say about Olovia? Of course she's getting a little old for us—what about Marilyum, did you try her snatch? But Claude's got a little tired, sated after four years of it, he's out traveling around the country looking to refresh himself with a few country girls. It won't take long. He's just passing through, as the saying goes. Have you seen his car? Woo-woo, eh, Claude? Yes, Claude has changed a lot in the last few years. Haven't we all. Vivien has. Yes, Vivien has changed in many ways. Would you believe it, she used to be a quiet, almost an abnormally passive child. I can remember her in her crib, no more than a few months old. She used to lie in there staring up at the air with her big dark eyes, not making a sound, just staring with those eyes, waiting for me to come in and pet her. Then she'd fall asleep and stay asleep all night, until I came in and petted her again. She was always like that, all through girlhood—a strange, passive, loving child. She used to let me do anything I wanted to . . . ''

"Drink, Paul. Drink!"

Paul looked at her blankly, as though her words had got stuck somewhere in his brain and he was waiting for his heart to pump them through, but now his wandering hand poured another drink and he looked down at that. "She used to let me do anything . . . " It was whispered in sadness, from the past. Whatever else Paul was preparing to say was interrupted by a soft windy noise. Claude looked toward Mrs. James's end of the table, found her looking over her spoon at him. She pursed her lips and blew at him. Claude smiled and nodded his head. Mrs. James blew again. Now he looked to Vivien.

"She wants you to eat."

"Ah, I had a late lunch," Claude said to Mrs. James, and for an instant she managed to look almost sorrowful. Smiling he ate some stew. "It's very good," he said.

Mrs. James smiled, and her look went briefly to Vivien before she bent to her food again, hungrily.

Vivien stood up, taking her dish and Claude's to the kitchen with her. As soon as she had gone Paul put down his glass, banging it. He leaned his head upon that hand, while the other hand, whether with intent or not, slid stiffly across the polished table toward the knife. At the last moment his palm skidded out from under him and hit the knife, sending it sharply to the floor. Almost it seemed that Paul didn't know what he had done, for he questioned Claude in little lopsided circles that didn't hold any one thing in view for long, i.e. what, what was that? Claude did not say, and Paul reached out that slippery hand to Claude's. Patting Claude's hand he blinked at him, slowly at first, soon rapidly. "Claude, she cares," he said, blinking tears away. "She really cares!" Then he fell on his crapulous face, his hair trailing out toward his empty fifth, his silk-sleeved left arm sunk in stew. Withdrawing his hand from Paul's, Claude studied him with distaste, unable to decide which repelled him most, the earlier Paul or this final one who had let all that wickedness dissipate in puling maudlinese. Had he, when he knew that he was passing out, acted cunningly to spare himself being nailed there to the table with his knife between his shoulderblades? Claude still had not decided when Vivien returned, without dessert. How viciously she closed the knife, how lightly she placed it on the table top! Between them they heaved Paul up and dragged him, it was like trying to manipulate a huge water-filled inner tube, to the couch. He landed on his face. Vivien pulled off a boot, dropped it on the floor, leaving the other one. Claude turned the mouth toward air. Then they straightened up to look at one another, or at the space between, and for a moment he was afraid she might try to apologize.

"I'll have to get Mother off too. It won't take long."

"Well . . . " He would have reached out and touched her, but did not feel he was close enough to do it gracefully. "It's getting late. Maybe we should give up tonight."

"Where are you staying—at the Frontier, room 606?"

He laughed. "No, I'm in a little hole down south."

"Tell me where."

"What about tomorrow, do you work tomorrow?"

She stepped closer to him now, her evasive eyes trying to meet his, not quite in friendliness or even trust, but with unimaginable hopes, like an animal's. "You have changed, haven't you?"

[85]

Laughing again he touched her hair. "I'm out of uniform. Do you work tomorrow?"

"I don't have to."

"Yes, I'll pick you up after work. What time do you get off?"

"Five."

"I'll be there then."

"Will you?" Her arms felt very warm around his neck, her face was damp, and beneath his hand the heat of her scalp seeped through her hair. "You will?"

"I'll see you at five," he said, standing rather stiffly while she made a pact of it.

"You have cool lips." She touched them with her fingertips.

"Oh?" Not waiting to ask her what that meant, good or bad, he pecked her forehead with his cool lips and moved smiling, saluting into the hall. "I'll see you," he said, but she did not answer him, or even accompany him to the door, choosing a time like this to show restraint. Was he supposed to wonder if they were friends?

But closing the door he felt, without relief, that he must be made of flint. He had driven five hundred miles to visit her, and at first chance had run away. While she, by silently letting him go, had left him with a picture of her standing in that hideous room, watching him, that showed her to be equally cruel. So, he could say, it was a trap, and he was well out of it. He was suffering only the usual, suicidal pangs that any parting left him with, he having never learned how to say goodbye. Perhaps he was made of flesh. Driving the foolish beast back into town, he thought a drink at the Frontier might put some blood, or ichor, in his veins.

The bar was busier than it had been four years ago. He could not have his corner stool but had to settle on a central one beside a perspiring couple who held themselves austere until he had ordered his drink, then fell again to crucifying an old pal named Max, and on his other side by a man who looked as though he knew all about mortgages but wanted to tell someone about politics. Whenever the waitress ran over for a glass of draught beer she jogged Claude's arm, after first crying furiously "Excuse me sir!" Thus Claude, drinking gin, found himself alone with his mean thoughts again. He hoped Vivien had appreciated his tact in not setting himself up here at the Frontier, in room 606. He hoped she understood that he had wanted to be less direct, crass this time, that it did not bespeak less desire for her. He hoped she did, for at this point he could not say, himself. He backed off the stool and went to the telephone, where he was astonished to find that he still had Joanne Bancroft's number in his head.

"Well?" a big voice asked.

"Excuse me, sir." Claude hung up. Joanne Bancroft. At eleven-thirty on a warm Friday night, what had he been dreaming of? He continued on out of the hotel, stopping at the drugstore for a little O-O-O, an opener, on his way to the car. At the cabin he kicked off his painful shoes and slipped the few crystals of ice from the shuddering box into a beer, drank this one off to Paul. Then he lay down on the bed with the two others, to think. What he thought was that he had come an unconscionable distance to get hard up. Yet he had little chance to feel sorry for himself: he saw her standing there watching him leave, saw her wheeling Mrs. James away to some back room, taking herself off next, and, in the morning, awakening. He might have fallen in love with her right then, for pity, if he hadn't fallen asleep.

But in the morning he was awake much too early, brushing his teeth with lavender soap, packing his things, leaving his key in the door, leaving MRS WHITES

[87]

snoring in No. 1. He stopped for breakfast, warm coffee, warm orange juice, to clear his head, went back to the car with his soggy mind made up. Passing through town he looked to neither right nor left, not knowing exactly where her office was, but in the open country he looked everywhere and turned one of the radios on to wash away thought. A few minutes later he turned it off and turned around, not ready yet to cross over the pimply mountain he had reached. He would at least have to call her, there were no phones out here. Back in town he stopped instead at the new glass bank, chose the least popular teller of them all, to cash a savings bond. She was a witch but, what was worse, he was no patriot. Humbled, rich, he drove to Pascua next, for here too he would find no phones. Here a few pale faces were already looking about the plaza, at the little church, at the adobe huts, at one another most. He stood with them for an hour in the sun nursing a red soda pop, not wanting it but not wanting either to put it down unfinished before that watching girl, dash her joy at such a sale. There was a murmur as the maestros, led by children, came out of the church carrying the candlestick and carried it over to the cross and lighted the three candles it held. They went back in the church again and everyone looked at one another a little less furtively now. But there was another half hour's wait before the masked chapeyekas came prancing in from somewhere with a ridiculous little doll Judas, dressed like themselves in disreputable clothes, tied to the back of a stiff old mule; Pete, a grotesque caricature of a cop from both Arizona and Mexico who had spent some time in Arivada too, waving some burning, stinking rags on the end of a stick and urging the clowns to ever wilder antics as they set Judas on a throne of kindling wood beside the cross and danced in and out, around, around, embracing him. Claude waved at Pete as he danced by, but Pete turned his back on him and hopped

[88]

away, acting humorous. They hadn't thrown the flowers at him yet. Soon the chapeyekas skipped derisively off somewhere and Claude slunk back to the beast.

One thing he held against the bird force was the curse of knowing always which direction he was headed in, without the vaguest idea where he was going. He headed east this time, recalling as if it were yesterday every fifth or sixth mile of the road, where they hadn't torn it up, straightened it, bent it, laid it down again, and bordered it with regular houses planted eave-to-eave like an impenetrable, multicolored fence—soon a flag will wave from every antenna, we'll peek out at the savage world from a plaster fortress, nationwide. At 22.2 miles from town he turned onto a broken road, no longer oiled, past faded signs of warning, welcome, instruction, warning again, past benches where hitchhikers no longer sat beneath big signs that told the drivers where they wished to go or pretended to. Finding the front gate locked he took off across the sand, along the wire fence, until he came to a small hole in the southeast corner that had not changed. Wriggling through, he was pleased to find he had put on no weight that he could not see. The wide-necked whistle-blowers had never agreed that he could keep his figure in his own way, without exercise, but had kept on until the final dogged day trying to give him theirs. As he walked the rows of faded white buildings, stopping occasionally to read the faded notices on bulletin boards, broken glass crunched loudly beneath his shoes. He sought it out, refining it. They had removed all the portable valuables, the fieldlights, the wheel blocks, even the steel control tower, to the big new field, leaving only the outmoded and cumbersome. But on the edge of the runway the tattered windsock, once a matter of life and death, still flapped on its pole like a condom hung up to dry and forgotten long ago. The hospital was there, the heartless post office, the officers' club, the n.c.o. club, but all badly

[89]

beaten, weary, ready to cave in any day, the bowling
dlley first of all. In another few years the field would be
aesert again, albeit fenced. The plot of lawn in front of
h.q. which he had trimmed with clippers one Saturday
afternoon, in expiation of accumulated crimes he could
not now recall, was tumbleweed. He tossed a stone at
the sign above the door, still the brightest sign of all,
but at the shocking clatter looked the other way. Now,
unobserved, he went inside. They had left one desk
behind; he saluted it. "Good morning, Colonel," he
said, with soft respect. "Keep your pecker up." Slouching out he found his old mess hall, but wasn't hungry
now, perhaps in a little while he would drop over to the
p.x. for a beer. He found the building in front of which
he had stood in the sun all day waiting to be discharged,
in which the crazy doctor had suggested that he stay
over another day to let him check that heart again and
it had taken precious time to persuade the man that joy
alone made it beat so wild. Perhaps someday he would
die of that. He visited the movie theater next, but
Betty Grable was no longer there. So he walked crunching to his barracks, crunching in and up the stairs, past
the disconcertingly uneven rows where lay two-deep
the ghosts of ghosts, to his old corner bunk, up top.
Someone had carted his sack away, so he scrounged
old John's from down below. Old John wouldn't mind.
Old John Who? Old John Who and So What, he thought,
not wanting to think back to those wasted years, over
those that had come after them. "Wake me at four,
John," he said.

Old John was as unreliable as ever, of course; it was
four-thirty by the time Claude got back to the car and
turned the radio on, yet he did not hurry to town.
Drifting in he stopped at a little drugstore near the bus
depot. This was a store he had used once before, and now,
as then, there was no mannish clerk around. In fact the
girl he requested his trojans of looked like the same who

had waited on him all those years ago, but she did not seem quite so tickled today. He changed his order to the jumbo economy pack, that he might not have to trouble her again. By now she profoundly disapproved of him. She did not give his change to his outstretched hand, but sprinkled it on the titty mat, and she did not ask him if there would be anything else. "Tempus fugit," he reminded her going out the door.

He found Vivien's office easily enough, by five, and parked in front he mused the fact that she would find him for the first time not only not drinking but cold sober too. To himself he offered this as his apology for being here, since he seemed in need of one. He wished he had had time for a couple of beers, time to think this out.

"Hello," she said.

Graciously he opened the door for her. "Hop in." Somehow it made him feel better to see that she wore her same scarlet dress. "Have I been waiting long?"

"I wasn't going to ask that," she said, seated rather far away, rather stiff and childlike, undistinguished on red leatherette. "Nor whether you had a nice time today. The only thing I'm curious about is how it happens that you're still in town, but I wouldn't be so gauche as to ask you that."

Grinning, too gauche to smile, he offered her a cigarette. "I thought I'd stick around to find out whether you smoke."

"I don't."

So he took one himself and then drove through the anxious traffic in apparent funk, almost as though they did this every day, were bored with one another and nobody was watching them. The truth was that they were attracting wildly eager stares and glares, and he was having to steer the beast very carefully among those that went out of their way to challenge her and those that pulled over to the curb at sight of her. The truth also was that little Vivien, however unbending and far away, was somehow sending him more than the ordinary electricity. "Hi," he said.

"Where are we going?" she asked sociably. "To the Frontier?"

"No, I've had enough of the past. Since you ask, I had a lousy day. I thought we'd try one of those new glass houses I saw on the way into town last night."

"Oh let's," she said, to seem enthused. "I've never been to those. I've never been out of town."

So he stopped at the first of them, a frigid hothouse whose front tipped forward over the street in defiance of gravity, taste, and ordinance; inside, the tender day-time flowers could be seen huddling in family groups beneath a constant, unseen sun, and behind them was the hermetic door to the dark Cactus Room where the shy nocturnal plants, genus cereus, could bloom in privacy at any hour. Vivien, once out of the car, appeared less constrained. She did not have that stiffness so many have on first entering bars, that air of waiting stubbornly for alcohol to loosen them, which so often presages their manner when it comes time for bed. She was already excited when the martinis came. She remembered very vividly their first meeting, had been looking forward to this reunion for years, she said, had he? She gave him no time to answer this, and she nibbled her olive while she talked. "I suppose you know now why I didn't show up at the Frontier that night."

"Well, how is he today?" Claude asked.

"Were you very angry with me?"

"No," he said, trying to remember how he had felt. "But that's all past."

"You knew I wanted to come?"

"I couldn't be sure of course. But I'd caught a glimpse of his face in the car that night, and I didn't know you very well . . . "

"You thought I was a spineless little idiot who could

be talked into or out of anything by anyone," she said, putting down her glass but at once picking it up and drinking from it.

"As a matter of fact," he said, "I thought you were a sometimes wise little idiot who probably did the right thing by standing me up."

"I'd have been there early if it hadn't been for brother snake."

He smiled. "Maybe brother snake was right."

"I'm here tonight."

"Maybe you're right this time," he said, and drank. "Let's say so. Let's talk about something else."

"One more question: *did you wait very long for me?*"

"When?"

"That night?"

It seemed to him that he had given her fifteen minutes and then had gone, with relief, to call up Joanne. "Yes," he said. "Say, I'm glad to see that you drink."

She took up her martini and, only slightly wryfaced, gulped it off, excused herself while he ordered another one. Tipping backward into the dark soft embrace of the booth he watched, really watched her go. She walked as though she wanted him to. She did have fine legs, slender, straight, and used them well to toss the short skirt that flaired from her firm backside, left-right, left-right, like the flicking tail of a little red virgin squirrel in heat. He found himself still looking at the door when she came out. Now her thighs broke out by turn beneath her skirt as though they said, watch—watch—watch—watch—what I'm bringing you, and sitting down again with her he felt her electricity pass through him as though their thighs were joined underneath the table with nothing at all between to insulate. The same thing had happened four years ago, when she first approached. He had received the shock from many others before, a few afterward, but never to quite the same degree. What always surprised him was that he could not remember a single one of those girls who wasn't prettier than Vivien (he recalled that night's conceit: to be seen with her or to be stood up, either horn would wound his vanity) but now all at once her appeal seemed not so very surprising after all. The others, it seemed to him, had wanted him as much as he had wanted them, at most, while Vivien was obsessed with the idea of having him. "Hi," he said, but now looking at her he saw that she had turned green, chartreuse. "Are you all right?"

"Very," she said, and a more agreeable color washed her face. "The first drink always does that to me. Now I'm anesthetized and ready for anything."

"Shall we go outside for a breath of air?"

"Anything but that," she said, drinking emphatically; when the glass came down she was in full bloom again.

"My God," he suddenly laughed, patting her hand, "and here I was lolling here, watching you go and come, imagining it was passion that made you walk that way!"

She withdrew her hand, but her deepsunk turquoise eyes held his briefly, a rarity, swept lightly over his face and lingered on his lips, he felt, before they withdrew again. "It was," she said, replacing her hand rather awkwardly next to his on the table.

He ordered another drink. "Tell me some more about brother snake."

She used that awkward hand to pick up her drink and finish it. "I want to hear about you," she said, her slender fingers spinning the empty glass. "I want to hear everything you've done since I saw you, everything you've done since you left the army, everything you did while you were in the army, everything you've done all the way back to the first thing you can remember, and everything you want to do for the rest of your life."

Well. Handing her glass aside to the waitress he

smiled and, "Claude Squires," he said.

"No, I mean it, Claude."

"So do I."

"Well, God damn it then, don't talk," she said, hunching forward to peer at her fresh drink as though it were her heart that lay pierced, embalmed in it. "Don't bore me—I'll bore you. I'll be twentyone years old next week, I've been working for six years, and I've earned the right to tell someone who I am and what I think. First I worked three years to put Paul through engineering school, until the navy took him off my back. Every week I'd send him a check for thirty dollars, saving out just enough of my check to buy groceries for Mother and me, and pay the rent—we lived in a one-room apartment then. Oh, it wasn't so hard, that was simply the thirty dollars the other girls spent on their clothes. I got so that I hated clothes, and I hated all working girls. Clothes were all that I could see in them, and mine were as much as they cared to see of me. I still get a little ill whenever I see a new pair of shoes. But Paul had what he needed, all the clothes and the books and the booze, and I was supposed to find solace in that. The trouble was that I had long ago lost all interest in Paul. Ever since we were children Paul got everything, whatever he wanted, and always from me. . . . There's more, there's more—but we'll wait for that. I could never afford to do anything about this disgusting tooth," she said, pointing it out to him. "Ten dollars would have been enough ten years ago. It will cost fifty now."

"I like your tooth," Claude said. "It lends character to your smile, if you ever smile."

"I'm going to have it fixed next week, for my birthday," she said, with lips compressed. "Then I'll smile. You came a week too soon."

"I like your tooth."

"It's been like this since I was ten, since it was new,"

Vivien said. "I got it trying to convince a little girl that my mother wasn't dumb. 'Deaf, not dumb,' I used to yell at them, '*Deaf* NOT DUMB!' Well, as you see, I'm working for myself these days. I've been working for three years to have this tooth fixed and put myself through school, and by fall I should have enough saved for one year. My freshman year," she said, pausing to pour her martini down.

"Where do you plan to go?"

Passing her glass mockingly aside to him she said, "I don't know, maybe to Paris, maybe to New Zealand or Australia or Canada, probably to the University of Mexico, wherever they have something besides engineers. You see, I want—there must be a more polite way of putting this, but the blunt fact is that I want to be a poet. All right, I am a poet, I write poems. It's very funny," she said, and remembered not to smile, "five years ago I used to think all poets thought noble thoughts and kind, walked in beauty like the night, and wiped whenever necessary their behinds on fleecy clouds that Phoebus sent. I had no idea that poems could be written from life, by living people, here and now. Out east seventyfive years ago perhaps, in England or France or even Germany, but not here in the baby state, certainly not a love poem called 'The Offal ones,' by an ugly little girl who lives with a snake. How do we ever come by subversive things like this, out here? I know we all want to leave something behind besides offal, but how does the way ever come to us here, certainly not through the newspapers or the chamber of commerce or the school or even the library. Sometimes I think the wild animals carry it, the way they carry rabies and a few still carry bubonic plague. Or maybe the cactus. Maybe the crazy trees prick it into us with their thorns. Maybe the Indians brought it with them over the Bering Sea. But that isn't what I want to go to school to learn, not 'poetry.' I'd like to be a general practioner like William Carlos Williams, only in Labrador. I'd like to be Schweitzer, a missionary to the body and soul, in Biloximiss or Evanstonill. I'd like to be Gandhi anywhere. I think I'll take everything in the catalogue from anthropology to zoology, except engineering, accounting and salesmanship. And typing— I know how to type." She bent her head over the new drink the waitress had brought, so far over that her heavy hair, held loosely by a colorless ribbon behind her ear, fell forward from her shoulder onto his hand and hers. "Do you want to come too?" she asked of the little green heart in there, apparently his this time.

"I'd love to," he said, leaving his hand beneath her hair. "Let's go to Mexico. I'll study anthropology and archeology, minor in treasure hunting. I met a man yesterday who knows where some treasure is. We'll help him find it and then we'll all live in the future like in the past only a little better. . . . Oh well."

"What else?"

"That's all."

"Then stop boring me," she said, and he watched her nibble his heart, after first sucking the clotted blood from it. "I'm trying to tell you all my plans and you aren't listening. Don't you see, this is the time for me to leave if I ever will. Mother doesn't need me any more —she's had her fifteen miles a day from me for ten years now. Does that sound heartless?"

"No," he said, "my mother's in a nut house."

"Paul could afford to hire a strong nurse for her, someone strong enough to also drag him to the couch at night." She hadn't heard him. "Maybe she'll even have the kindness to bury his knife in him, I never could. You see how it is, I've outlived my usefulness to them. I've got to leave. It would be better for everyone. All I need is someone to push me out of the door, choose some direction to head me toward." Vivien finished her drink and said, "That's where you come in."

"I do?"

She would not look at him. "I've told you I'm going

to be twentyone years old next week," she said. "Twentyone is too old to go anywhere alone, you know that. I want to go with someone. I don't mean as a bride, I'm not so gauche as that, but as a mistress or paramour or concubine or companion or friend or pal or anything else. I just don't want to be left alone! I want to get out of here!" She said it again for all the wide-faced flowers to hear: "*I want to get out of here!*"

"All right, let's go," he said, and they stood up. She remembered to take her big black purse, walked fairly well on her ballet toes, but a couple just outside the hermetic door looked twice before entering the Cactus Room, and then the man had to shove his lady hard to make her go in. Claude, a gentleman likewise, located and shouldered another door, glass and ass-backwards, and the cool evening air hit Vivien first. She took two little ballet steps and she was laughing drunk. Claude was drunk. They rode the drunken beast down the street laughing at the party sounds she made, at all the tipsy glass houses along the way and all the drunks going in and out of them who paused to blink as they partied by, until a patrol car blinked, and in that sudden silence blinked again. It was night. Claude turned on his lights, the patrol car cruising slowly by. That was a friendly cop, they both agreed, and Vivien waved back at him. Claude turned in at the first glass restaurant, guided the beast around to the back, where the shrimps were fried and the coffee was drunk in the life-giving air. They ate without talking, martiniated. But a few minutes later, wiping their chins, they looked enquiringly at one another, for it was scarcely seven-thirty and their evening felt over. "Well, that was my idea," he said. "Have you another one?"

They could think of nothing interesting and time-consuming. They did not feel like drinking or dancing or even sitting still at an outdoor movie, so they dragged the streets in search of inspiration. They headed south.

She did not mention the Frontier in passing, nor did he point out MRS WHITES to her. At the city limits she snuggled up to him, tucking her warm hands beneath his leg. "Let's go exploring," she suggested, nosing his neck through her hair. "They say there are all sorts of little towns where people used to live."

"How far are they?"

"Oh miles and miles over unpaved roads."

"Let me put it another way—what time do you have to get back tonight?"

"I don't *have* to do anything," she said, withdrawing her hands. "Or as you put it, let me put it another way. I could make love all night if you'd like me to. All day too."

"Ah." He stopped for gas, trying to think while the damned bell bonged. The attendant, a fussy philatelist, was still counting them out when Claude pulled away. As soon as they were on the road again he began his speech, whatever it was going to say. "I don't want to sound stuffy," he said with a self-exploratory laugh, "but won't you be missed?"

Vivien said, "I called Paul just before I left the office and told him he'd have to make dinner tonight and very likely breakfast in the morning."

He began again, saying, "I don't want to sound over-cautious, but somehow I don't feel very impulsive right now. Of course I'd like very much to make love with you. I didn't drive fivehundred miles to attend the Easter Ceremony, or revisit Tipton Field. You're an attractive girl and I like the way you express yourself, I like the way you flick your tail when you're walking away, and I like the way your thighs seem to want to break out through your dress when you approach. I'd like to see what else they do. But that doesn't say I'm thinking of getting married yet, far less going back to school. I'm not anything like that regular yet. You may be right that I've changed, but not that much, I'm still a tramp. For all I know I may always be. I'm afraid you think that going to bed with a man changes him, some dream like that. It isn't true. Oh, it changes him in some ways—I can remember how soft and warm you are, just from that little while we had—but hell this isn't any good. I don't seem to be able to make up my mind whether I'm telling you off or seducing you. Four years ago I wouldn't have bothered with any of this.''

"Dear Claude,'' she said as though she were beginning a little blue letter to him, "why don't you shut up and do what you used to do.'' She made it easier for him this time, in that when he put his arm around her he did not have to lift up her skirt, or slip his hand up underneath to reach her thighs where they lay gently kissing one another above her tight silk stockings. They were soft, still soft, and warm despite the chilly night. He rolled his window up. She was wearing a garter belt, a silk slip it seemed, and that was that. "Bear right at the next intersection you come to,'' she said, and she did not take his hand away, or breathe, when he obeyed.

Thus they almost missed their turn, the beast responding loathly to Claude's one hand and almost rocking them out the door, rocking them the other way as Claude spun the wheel full circle to miss an on-coming car, and for an uncertain hundred yards they were tossed loosely together as Claude fought to keep her to the road. When he could he glanced at Vivien, to smile; apparently she had seen none of it, her eyes were closed. This was a lesser road, older and narrower and with no white lines, with fewer cars. For a while they slid peacefully toward the moon, until Vivien told him to turn again, left this time and onto sand. He drove a half mile farther and stopped the car, turned to look down at her. "Hey.''

She opened her eyes to him, surprised, yet she kissed him readily enough, but kindly, as though this were a game she no longer really enjoyed. He saw that he had reacted too easily to the schoolboy stimuli, car, radio, moon, sideroad, but she would refuse to be thus conventionally dated by him, whatever else she wanted it was much too late for this. He had little patience too, but as a mocking gesture of propriety he kissed her once more anyway. "What's the matter, Viv, are my lips still cool?"

"Yes. They're supposed to be. A woman's are supposed to be warm."

"Yours are warm."

"Then everything's all right," she said.

So they drove again, Vivien sitting up and looking now, but as navigator only, letting the desert scratch its own thorny poetry on the enormous moon. "You seem to know where we're going," Claude said to her. "I thought we were exploring."

"I know where we're going."

"You've been here before?"

"No. I have a roadmap pinned on the wall beside my bed. I study it at night. Don't you like the road I chose?"

"Very mu-much."

"What then, are you worried about your car?"

"She isn't mine."

"Oh well then."

"She belongs to a woman in Oklahoma," he said, gunning noisily.

"Oh well then," she said, but she looked around her at the beast. Now she advised him of his next two turns and snuggled up to him again. He found the first of them, but he had begun to wonder a little by the time she sat up and said "Turn around."

He turned around and hastened back to an ancient cattleguard, from which a trail climbed north or east up a little hill, then east or south along the top. "There it is," she said, of the sprinkled lights below. Either she was a crazy romanticist òr her roadmap was very old. Two miles away, one mile beyond the town, the night was cleanly perforated by a perfect stream of cars. Watching her arrange her dress, he had little doubt that her map was new. "Well done," he said patting her. They crept down the hill, over another cattleguard, onto a once-but-only-once-paved road that ran between two dark hills of slag, around a dark railroad station, into what remained of town. The grocery and the drugstore-bar had lights inside, the church was white, but the pool hall and the movie house were sadly closed. The jail was closed.

"There's supposed to be a hotel somewhere."

"Maybe they can tell us here," Claude said, drawing up before the Copper Castle Arms. He got his suitcase from the trunk and they squeezed past the heavy door, into a long narrow room lighted only at the distant end. There was a fine old rug on the floor, a rocking chair, and in one dark corner a huge copper pot of dead, very tall bamboo. There was a desk, which they reached by following a diagonal track across the rug, and it had a bell on it. Nothing happened the first time Claude rang, but at second ring a cockroach scurried to a nearby door. Presently an old man came out, wiping his hands on a big blue handkerchief. He was halfway to the desk before he looked up, backed off at sight of them. But he recovered well, and he tucked his handkerchief carefully in his shirt pocket as he approached. "I was just thinking to take a bath and go to bed," he said.

"Ah," Claude said for apology. "We were wondering if you have a room for tonight?"

The man looked here and there behind his desk, fussing with his handkerchief. He handed Claude a bit of pencil, blunt end first. "Here, you can write on this," he said, smoothing out on the desk for him a brown newspaper wrapping, from Iowa. Mr. V. O. Castle turned to his keyboard while Claude wrote. "You're young," he said. "You won't mind a little climb."

"Oh no."

"I'll give you the fourth floor. That'll be quieter."

"Fine."

"Well, let's see, I'll give you 402. That's directly connected with the bath."

"Oh fine," Claude said, accepting the key to 402. "How much will that be?"

"Here's your towel and soap," Mr. Castle said, handing a big towel and half a bar of soap to Vivien.

"Thank you," Vivien said.

"How much do I owe you, sir?"

"Now did I give you your key?"

"Yes, you did."

"I gave you your soap," he said to Vivien.

"Yes."

Claude dropped his ten dollar bill on the desk, and the old man picked it up absently. "Well, you go straight up those stairs and straight on up. You'll find 402 right at the top."

They turned toward the stairs, Claude with his key, Vivien with her towel and soap.

"Now don't forget your bag!"

"Oh no."

He waited until they were well up the stairs before he turned out the light. "Have a nice sleep."

"Thank you," they both called back.

It was fine that the moon was out, it shone through the high narrow window, lit up some of the high narrow stairs ahead, showing them how to pace themselves. There was no bulb at all on the second floor, a tiny one on the third, none on the fourth. Claude's second match found 402, directly in front of them. His fingers found the lock, but his patience was scarcely up to it. At last it turned, and he turned the knob only to find that he had locked them out. He had to put his bag down and find the door again, find the lock. Claude entered first. Well that he did, for something heavy and sharp smacked his eye, swung back and smacked it again, perhaps blinding him. Groping for it, now a wildly elusive thing, he discovered it to be a two-inch nut suspended in the air by a heavy cord. He jerked and they were in blinding light, painful light, that glared from a great bulb screwed high in the ceiling at the distant end of the narrow room, directly above the big white, white-quilted bed. Shading his eyes, he placed his bag on the floor beside the chair. "What in hell is the name of this place?"

"Perhaps," she said.

He watched her go over to the dresser, where she looked only briefly into the mirror, making little or no attempt to arrange herself. She stooped to drawers, beginning oddly with the lower one, working up, until she came out with a red pen from one of the little drawers up top. She examined the pen, tested its cruddy point on her finger tip. There was no ink, but she had no one to write to anyway; she replaced it and turned to look at Claude. Smiling he sat down on the chair, stood up again, for she leaned there rather awkwardly, with-drawn, as though she were back in the car at five o'clock. He too, he saw in the mirror in back of her. He started forward with the idea of kissing her, but halfway there he stopped. He smiled at her. "I guess I'll go use that soap," he said.

"All right." She danced past him, on her toes. "Now don't forget that towel!" she said.

"Oh no," he said, taking it from the bureau top. Whoever designed the Copper Castle Arms seemed to have looked forward to a day when there would be a shortage of lateral space around Perhaps: the bathroom, through a door beside the bed, was also high and narrow, with barely standing space before the stool and outside the tub. Claude was gratified to find that this thought-ful man had installed the most beguiling of frivolities, a shower head, copper-green, discus-size, piped to the ceiling fifteen feet up. He stripped before fooling with

it. Seconds later, perched on the stool, he had had his
shower, but decided to wait there awhile in hope of a
warmer one. Pressure built quickly, or Mr. V. O. Castle
had finally filled his tub: Claude was no longer safe
anywhere, not even splayed midair between the stool
and the hall doorknob. He was stretching forward to
his clothes, to hang them with the towel on the door,
when it swung out and he found himself teetering,
flailing space over Vivien. He tipped back against the
smooth and shocking wall just in time to save them both.
"Take the towel—take my clothes," he yelled at her,
for she had had the good sense to leave her own outside.

He watched her hang his shirt and pants on either
side of the mirror, spread his socks and shorts on the
dresser top, and bend to place his shoes on the floor
soles-up. Now he watched her hang the towel on the
dry side of the door, step tentatively inside with her
arms crossed and shivering in front of her. Climbing
down he said, "So you want a shower too."

"I thought I did."

They stood before one another with stiffly chattering
grins. Yet they found themselves not so very cold, were
in fact growing acclimated. He climbed over the side
of the tub, helping her in. Now he had to hold onto
her while he reached out for the soap, and she helped
bring him back. By mutual consent, since he had the
soap, he washed her first, beginning with her back and
working his way down and around, soaping her everywhere well. He began to see why she hated clothes.
She was lovely. Her thighs he already knew, but now
he could study the rest of her. She had a small pattable
tail. Her breasts, round and high, were no less than
they'd seemed to be, under the circumstances a big
surprise. He liked the punchiness of her round belly, not
quite a pot, and the way it flattened out to her ribs.
Soon it had a little white beard on it. Her thighs he
already knew and he kissed each of them now, after

rinsing first. They were in no mood at all for the slippery ceremony of Exchanging Soap. It fell, of course, and laughing she backed rudely into him as she stooped for it. She too washed thoroughly, beginning as he had in back, soaping well. But it seemed that he was more ticklish than she, he squirmed. Soon he was laughing with delight that she should choose such a way to hold him still, but she would not let go and finally he had to slip from her grip. He grappled the soap away from her, held her at arm's length while he rinsed. He turned her around, both of them half-drowned with laughing soap, pinioned her arms behind her back. Her hair, pinched behind her head in a rubber band, hung straight down her back in a dark rat tail. He tugged on it, turning the shower off. Then he leapt from the slippery tub to the slippery floor.

"Save some towel for me!"

He tossed the towel in to her, stood before the mirror rubbing himself not very briskly with his soggy shirt. His nightclothes at least were waterproof, or so guaranteed: he tossed the wet box of them under the bed as Vivien ran into the room, half-entoweled. "You'll catch pneumonia," she cried, running back again. "Get into bed."

She had already turned the covers back and he complied gladly, drawing the sheet to his chattering chin with one hand, with the other shading his eyes from the bright spotlight overhead. When she came out at last her hair hung almost dry, almost down to her strapless silk slip that just did cover her centrally. "Hey, Jesse James!"

"Why Jesse?"

"Because you wear a mask over your beard."

"Did Jesse James have a beard?"

"I don't know," he said. "You do."

Laughing she lunged for the bed, stripped the sheet from him: he was as big as ever under there, which she seemed pleased to see. Now she lifted her mask an inch or two, curtsying nicely before she dove on him. Caught thus by surprise he tried to roll away—before he could do it her grasping fingers had become a glove, a warm and living glove that he knew he had never worn before although it seemed to know so intimately his measurements, even more intimately than the rubber one that very soon would have to take its place. But just now he was in no mood for changes, he lay stretched beside her, answering her curious smile with his, or blowing warm wind into the hair about her ear whenever she turned her head to look down at him, at other times twisting himself to look at her under the explorative fingertips of his free hand. His other arm she had pinned beneath her, but now she released it just enough for him to bend his head to her breast, only the nearer one, and together they watched it grow. She held him strongly there, while his lips sought out various ways to soften her, but not until he had his hand planted rudely between her thighs, as earlier in the car, did she let go, and then so utterly, flat on her back, her arms spread out so loosely at her sides, her legs spread out, her ridiculous little-girl slip high up about her neck, her eyes so placidly closed that he paused long enough to scare himself, had she passed out, or died? Here in Perhaps! But no, he could feel her thighs still alive, breathing alongside his wrist, and now he found her briefly tense behind until those muscles too went soft with all the rest. It seemed that she was ready at last for him to kiss her, everywhere, and he did, although he arrived slowly and circuitously; when he looked up her eyes were open just wide enough to look down at him. Seated back down he offered her something else to watch, since she did so avidly, but still it wasn't until he put his weight on her that she came all the way back from wherever she had been, instantly churning, heaving, bucking him as though to see if she would find a way out through him, or he in through her, which, which, which, which, and still was not sure even when he had to crush her, finally, with every ounce he had of weight and strength while she cried out. In the sudden peace that he imposed she quit, and they dove together into a warm deep bath they had prepared themselves of joy and pride in the heroic fight they'd fought, although with the cold tip of his mind that would not submerge he worried that she could have put up a longer one. But she floated up to kiss him weakly on the lips, as though to let him know that he had won. She was wrong, they both were dead. He tried, but could not move, not even for a cigarette. Someone else would have to roll him off.

No one had when he awoke sometime later to see a little pool of water sloshing in the warm hollow of her cruelly punched-in chest; he toppled over to his back. This woke her, and they met again, the strategy as before, Vivien attacking first, he next, then both at once, but this time she did not fight quite so hard. And afterwards he could get that cigarette, turn off that hellish light. Beside her on his back he knew that she too lay awake, probably watching him play lonely firefly in the dark, but he didn't feel like conversation unless she wanted it. After a little wait he snuffed out his cigarette on the handy window sill, and kissed her somewhere soft before he went back to sleep.

In the morning (or at least the sun was out) he opened to find her breasts watching over him close by, rather overweeningly it seemed to him, as though bursting with some secret they had enticed from him last night. But perhaps they had stared him awake for more progressive purposes. He made his smile polite, said "Good morning" before kissing them. This time he waited until she had lain down to die again, he had hung over her awhile, before he asked, "Jesse, are you dead?"

"Yes."

"What killed you?"

[108]

"I don't know."

"Can't you talk?"

"No."

"What do you want me to do to you?"

"You know."

"No, I don't," he said, arranging himself so as not to touch her anywhere. "No I don't. What?"

"You know," she said.

"What?"

"*Kiss me*," she said.

"Where?"

"Everywhere."

"Are you going to watch?"

"Yes."

"Not until you tell me why you die this way." It was difficult to avoid her writhing under him.

"I can't."

"Why not?"

"I can't!"

"Will you tell me afterwards?"

"Yes, all right. All right!"

So he did all he had before, and more, and when time came she put up her strongest fight of all; or perhaps she only made it seem that way to hide the truth that he had almost subdued her with all that talk, at any rate her climactic wail rang a little falsely in his ears. Kissing her once for bravery, he rolled over for a cigarette. Fired up, he cradled her in his arms and petted her. "Vivien?"

"Hi."

"Are you ready to tell me yet?"

"Tell you what?"

"Why you always want to die a while?"

"Wanting has nothing to do with it."

"Then why?"

"I don't know." She flung his arm aside and rolled away.

"Hey, you promised . . . " but she was already talking with her back to him.

"Once upon a time my father died. I was six, almost seven. Paul was twelve. Mother was hurt in the same accident. We stayed with an aunt and uncle that summer, until Mother was well enough to come home. 'Home.' They'd sold our house and found us a little blue apartment not far from theirs. My aunt came to stay with us, during the day at least. She would put us all to bed at eight, Mother in the livingroom, Paul and me in the bedroom, and then she'd go home. Mother had a little brass bell beside her bed, and Aunt Miriam would leave our door open so that we'd be sure to hear her if she rang. I suppose it didn't occur to her that Mother couldn't hear us, no matter what we did. We each had our own bed, separated by a folding screen— with four blue dragons chasing each other interminably around a bright red sun. On both sides, so that we both could see. They had four-clawed feet, red-forked tongues, and little red peepees between their rear legs, or at least that's what Paul said they were. He used to lie there telling me terrible stories about them until he was sure that Aunt Miriam had gone for good, and then he'd get into bed with me." Vivien stopped now, rolled over on her back, to gape at him.

"Yes?" he said, and it was a gape of hate as she turned away again.

"At bedtime Daddy always used to say," she said, " 'Aren't you going to give your brother a goodnight kiss?' I wouldn't though. I'd go over to Paul and turn my cheek to him. He'd kiss me, and my skin would creep. Daddy knew that I disliked Paul, and yet he used to say it every night. 'Aren't you going to give your brother a goodnight kiss?' And that's what Paul would say when he got into bed with me, 'Aren't you going to. . . ?' "

She stopped again, so he told her, "I used to kiss my sister too at night."

"You don't understand," she said, and he had difficulty hearing her now. "I used to wait for him. I would lie there waiting for him to get into bed with me, sometimes he'd even tease me by pretending to fall asleep and I'd have to call to him. It got so that he could make me do what he wanted first, for as long as he wanted it, and afterwards he would give me my goodnight kiss for it. . . . " She faced him again to stare.

"How long did it go on?"

"For years."

"Did he do anything else?"

"I used to ask him to," Vivien said, but only after he had looked at her again. "He never would. I don't think he ever will to anyone."

He made no comment, just now her point seemed an unimportant one. He lay beside her watching smoke rise very quickly from his nose, in a hurry to lose itself in this high old room, but then he felt her hand on him again and he put out the cigarette.

"Does it make your skin creep to be touched by me?"

Smiling, "Yes," he said, and they lay playing for a while, like hopeful six-year-olds. What you can. Soon they got up to take another shower, a somewhat more seemly one, and then they dressed. He kissed her damply, for friendship, before he packed.

At the mirror she said, "I wish we could stay here long enough to use all of those."

"What? So do I," he said, chucking the jumbo pack into his bag.

"But you'll find someplace else to use them, I'm sure."

He was waiting at the door for her to leave first. "Oh, lots of places," he agreed.

They met Mr. V. O. Castle on the second floor, coming up, and it startled him. But he smiled. "I was just thinking to come up and check whether you'd left," he said.

"We're just leaving now."

"You can't tell what's going on, way up there," Mr. Castle said.

"I guess you can't."

"You had a nice sleep though?"

"Oh, wonderful."

"That shower work O.K.?"

"Wonderfully."

"You didn't bring down your towel did you by any chance?"

"No, I'm afraid we left it there."

"Well, I'll go up for it later," Mr. Castle said, accompanying them back down the stairs. "Tomorrow will be soon enough. I guess I'll close up now and watch TV."

"By the way, what time is it?"

"Twelve noon," he said, holding his big door for them. "Sunday noon."

"Do you know of someplace where we could get some food?"

"Not right off," he said, considering. "I guess you're good and hungry, both of you?"

"Yes, we are."

"Well, Castle's Market is open sometimes on Sunday afternoon. . . ."

"That's the one up by the drugstore—or the bar?"

"No, that's not it. You turn east here and walk straight on down the street. You'll see it on your right. Or you can drive your car, just the way you're aiming there. She'll be down to open up any minute now. It's time she was."

Thanking him they stepped outside, and heard behind their backs the closing door, the sliding bolt. They drove their car. But they did not sit in it while they waited for Mrs. Castle to arrive on foot, they stood in the sun before the store, looking the other way as she approached. Soon they strolled over to the opened door, allowing her time to turn on the light, turn the OPEN sign around, before they stepped in. Now Mrs. Castle stepped out to look up and down the street, look again, as though wondering if her clock was fast, where was everyone? She soon came back to wait on them. When she saw that they were interested in the meat department, she turned on the other light; she sliced and weighed their country bacon exactingly, checked their fresh egg carton to make sure it was full, and with her apron flicked dust off their fruit cocktail can—it had been standing there much longer than the little ones, she had been saving it for them. She seemed surprised to hear that they had coffee in their car, but she was right about cigarettes. Matches too. It was Claude who happened to think of pepper. Ho, they had salt in their car, that was no surprise—Mrs. Castle came up with fresh bread, fresh country butter, JAM. She ceased at that, and when their purchases had been carefully scrutinized, padded, packed, she helped Claude pick up the precious sack, made sure he had a good hold on it. Vivien remembered spoons. Mrs. Castle, only briefly afluster, ran before them to the drygoods counter where after a little search she quickly tucked two wooden spoons inside their bag, ducked ahead of them to hold the door, nodding and smiling bashful acknowledgment as they filed thanking out. Vivien thought she heard her locking up.

They left Perhaps more or less as they had found it, back north over the little hill and down to the second cattleguard, onto one of several roads. Their choices in daytime seemed even more manifold, a bumper crop, their tires had left no distinctive marks, and Vivien seemed not to care at all whether Claude chose left or right. Soon finding that they had dug themselves a deep and hopeless track to the brink of a sandy wash, wadi size, they stopped for lunch. They prepared their fire, Claude collecting flat black stones from alongside the wash, Vivien snapping branches from the greasewood a few yards off, and then they paused. They thanked, after a moment of awful hunger, Mrs. Castle for giving them their fruit cocktail in the giant can, for they would be able to cook in that, after they had opened it. Claude praised the Cat for having left a screwdriver with Pete's pliers in the cubbyhole. Driving it with a rock, puncturing, hacking, prying, he worked off the lid. They ate their fruit cocktail as far as their wooden spoons would reach, and then they drank. Now—over Vivien's wail—Claude hacked out the bottom too, then sliced down one side, folded the edges up, handed Vivien an eight-by-ten-inch frying pan. She apologized for doubting him, so he found two rocks, one concave, one pestle-shaped, handed her two wildly scallop-edged tin cups which she set on the counter beside her stove. "Now get cooking," he ordered, and wandered off. But he didn't have to wander far to decide that all the water around Perhaps had been piped into the Copper Castle Arms last night.

"What have you been hunting?" she asked on his return. "Tyrannosaurs?"

"Tend your stove," he said, picking up the cups.

"What are you going to do with those?"

"Will you cook," he said, and went off to milk a water buffalo. Praise the Cat again for pliers, praise the office for a clean white shirt, he lay down and drew from her rusty teat two cups of warm and vaguely alcoholic liquid strained clear enough to see the bottom of the cup. He poured in all the coffee from his bag, not a little of the salt, and stirred well with a greasewood twig. Carrying his brew over to the stove, placing it up on back where it would not cool too fast, he said to Vivien, "Don't just stand there sniffing, get *dinner* ready."

Seated facing one another at the wadi's edge, their serving dish resting on a flat black stone between, they shared their bacon and eggs, he outsharing her by perhaps half a pound and eight-to-four, thus too busy to complain. She had fried some of the bread in bacon fat, and they ate that first, the rest with fresh country butter and strawberry jam. The heels they saved and shared to swab the remnant juices from their dish. She cooked a pretty good meal, outdoors. "Don't drink that coffee too fast, that's all there is," he warned, dumping his own sludge on a nearby rock and lying down for a cigarette.

It was a nice day for an outing. Well, the sun was out, and they were in a mood to be struck blind by it. And dumb. They lay, shoulder to shoulder, far apart. They tried to talk, but everything they thought to say could best be answered by yes or no, or both—or not at all. Were you surprised to hear from me? Yes, were you surprised to see me? Yes, but would you ever have thought to come if I hadn't written first . . . ?

"This reminds me of Sunday in New York," he said at last by way of apology. "My mother, fresh in from the country, would spend her feverish day showing us the metropolis. 'What a lot we're going to see today!' and my sister Claudine and I, who lived in it six months of the year, would smile yes for her and run to catch up with her, miles upon gaping miles around the windy corners of the block-sized department stores (it didn't matter a damn that they were closed) then into the babbling tea rooms for peas and carrots and cold croquettes, out again to the museums, the galleries, the biggest goddam globe you ever saw with colored lights blinking on and off all over it, the zoo, the zoo, or else the endless dog, the cat, the horse, the flower show where by God we stayed long enough to get our money's worth. Then, finally, a big Child's butterscotch sundae bust that I still gag on when time has come for the big whipcream Goodbye. My father on the other hand would spend his day with us discovering a famous country inn, where they brought you a tremendous bloody chicken to pick at with your peas, not ten minutes away from my mother's house. Then back to the car to speed, in those days, fifty miles an hour over the countryside which we were too low down and blacked out to see, and he joking, joking all the while to make it easier on whatever girl he'd brought along to show us to and show to us. (If it seems we spent our childhood away from home, 'visiting' in vehicles or on the run, it's almost true.) And from both sides came the crossfire of fancy questions which we both could spot as easily as you can see the tracer bullets in flak flying overhead—but at other times I see it as though it was we ourselves, Claudine and I, who were being fired back and forth, like tennis balls put by for weekend use—served up overhand but with a twist in hope that the receiver would flub his shot. 'Claudine, will you promise me not to get your hair mussed up, I don't want to have to curl it again tonight,' and then such tenseness whenever my father tousled it, rolled the windows down, or folded back the top. 'How's school going, pals? Well, maybe next year we'll send you to a good private school when you come to New York.' 'How many cocktails did your father have for lunch— well, *about*? . . . What, what did he say about Roosevelt . . . ?' and then her fiercely muddled cautioning not to believe all we heard, especially under the influence of alcohol. And there were a few old regulars like 'Where did you kids eat lunch today, pal. . . . Ah well, we'll fatten you up with steak tonight.' I tell you, I can still die a little when I see the sun start down, a long shadow on the ground, or a light turned on inside a house. Pretty soon it will be time to cry goodbye. Then you have thirty seconds to dry your eyes and smile hello again. Soon comes September, the biggest goodbye-hello of all. I love the summer and the dark." Vivien said nothing, so he went on, "The funny thing is that I sometimes still like upheaval, for upheaval's sake. That's funny, isn't it?"

[116]

"Yes," she said. So they lay for a while watching the falling sun, not low yet but well on its way past the meridian. Then they stood up to take a walk, Vivien pointing out dozens of fiercely living things underfoot, small animals and plants he had never seen before, and naming them. They found a big barrel cactus lying on its side, still half alive, and they dug a hole for it with rocks, deep enough that it wouldn't fall again. They had to use their hands to set it straight, since Claude had no belt, and that took time, was a pleasant pain. On a butte nearby the wash they found what Vivien took to be the site of an ancient Indian dwelling, at least a semi-permanent camp, and they spent some time collecting shards of unpainted, corrugated clay and tried half-heartedly to fit them into some semblance of a pot. Meanwhile Vivien found two broken arrow heads, a fine stone knife, Claude could not, so they gave up. They met once more on top of a cliff that they had climbed, in a small mining cave facing south so that the sun shone in, Vivien on the rocks and very strong. They returned to camp, Claude checking the water and oil, kicking the tires, while Vivien washed the dishes in sand. She insisted that he take them to Oklahoma with him, along with the rest of the strawberry jam. "You can eat it with the spoons," she said. I'm putting them in the glove compartment."

"Thanks."

They backed onto a track that someone else had made, followed that a while, turned onto a stronger one, a stronger, Vivien making the choices now, unerringly, to the hardtop road. They reached the main highway almost at once, it seemed, and here Claude slowed down, letting the homerushing traffic wash around them in ferocious waves that somehow could not touch them or catch them up, the beast herself seeming temporarily tranquilized by Sunday Brahms. By the time they saw the city ahead almost half its lights were on. Claude turned on his headlights, but quickly off again. "I can see better in the dark," he said, but by the time they reached the city limits he had them on. Even MRS WHITES was blinking blue. He stopped at the first restaurant with a big red cocktail glass on it. "O.K.?"

"O.K."

The booths were square, so he moved in with Vivien. "Hey, Viv," he said.

"You need a shave," she said, touching his chin.

He touched her skirt. "You need a press."

The waitress, offering doilies, smiled on them.

"Maybe we'd better have beer tonight?"

Vivien shook her head. "A martini will be fine."

They drank them fast, and Claude ordered two more when Vivien left. He was watching for her when she came out, even though the waitress was a sailing sex machine, and stood up to let her brush past him into the booth. "Hey Jesse, I wish we could go exploring again tonight."

"I wish we could too," she said before she sat down, but then, "I have to be at work at eight."

"We could probably make it by noon," he said. "Aren't you ever late?"

She smiled. "I have to get home to see how Mother is."

"I thought you didn't care anymore."

"I care."

"Well, O.K."

They ordered steaks, another martini first.

"Anyway," Vivien said, "you have business to attend to in Oklahoma, haven't you?"

"Yes," but after a glance at her: "I'm delivering that car for my old man."

She oh-ed, but did not look at him.

"God damn it, I feel awful," he said, setting down his drink. "Like a kid up before the teacher while she sits placidly waiting for him to recite a lesson he's supposed to have learned, but he doesn't remember what it is. Or he remembers, but he hasn't learned it well enough and doesn't want to make a fool of himself. She insists. She thinks it's stubbornness. . . . ''

Vivien snapped her yellow plastic olivestick. Then she reached over for his red one, snapping it. "He should obey his instincts—he's making a fool of himself," and her fingers made a square with the broken sticks. "We've had a good time and now you're spoiling it. Why don't you think about last night?"

He did for a minute, but "Tonight's another night."

"If you're worried about tonight, you can come back and get that waitress after you take me home. She looks nice."

"Sure I can," he said, "and won't that do us a lot of good?"

"It would do me good to know that you aren't lonely, Claude." She made it sound the truth!

"Well, aren't you a damned Samaritan."

"Let's stop."

"Let's."

They ate, they picked for a while at the tender parts, and then they had one more drink. A double one, the olive looked absurdly small inside. He dove for the bottom, got halfway there before he went numb. A minute later Vivien too came up for air, and they smiled again.

"You realize," he said, "I'll probably be passing back through again before too long."

"Fine."

"Meanwhile we can write."

"Let's not. Let's not make all these little arrangements, promises."

"Why do you say that?"

"I just hate to wait for anything."

"What do you want, telegrams?"

"No," she said.

They were down to their olives now, so he stood up and she followed him to the door. He held it wide, the car door too, slammed sharply when she was clear. Slamming his own he reached a hand toward her but drew it back. "No, you'd probably rather not." Since she did not say, he drove. It was a quiet drive, until they turned onto her stillborn street where not a single terrible blade of grass had changed. "I'll go in with you," he said.

"No, please, that's all right."

"I hate to think of you going in alone."

"Please don't worry. Paul probably passed out long ago with no one home to tell his stories to."

"Still, I. . . . "

"I'll give you a signal," Vivien said. "If everything's quiet, I'll turn my bedroom light on three times and leave it on. Watch the last window on the left." She leaned over for him to kiss her, but only politely and not for long. Patting his beard, she backed out of the car. "Goodbye," she said.

"Be good."

She started to leave, but came back to peer in at him. "Claude, don't forget the strawberry jam."

"I won't," he promised. He watched her run up the path to the door and, waving, go inside. Two lights were on, and soon a third came on, went off, came on, went off, came on. He watched for a few minutes longer, hoping to see some shadow of life behind the shade, and then he left. At the corner he stopped to look back at the bright orange window, but he did not have any of the kinds of boldness it would have taken to return to it.

Three

Instead he fled, capriciously, determinedly, like an ant making nonsense of an exacting map, through the moonstruck streets. For a while it seemed he was getting some place, but two more turns found him back at her house. Her light was off, which angered him, she might already be asleep, until he realized that he was on some other street. Abashed, resolved not to let this happen to him again, he began to pick his way more methodically, first left, then right, never the same way twice consecutively, in order that he could not possibly repeat himself. This was a game the Cat had played on Sundays, to pass time in such towns as Rye and High, make them seem interesting, which spoiled it now, for that was how the Cat had made it all through life, left right left right, let's see where we come out. Not he, not Claude. He chose to make conscious choices from here on out, and did, stopping at the corners to look for signs, take aim, before going on, and on and on, onto ever weaker roads fanning out like those desert tracks, but limply paved and ending abruptly in people's yards. He was lost. This made him furious, with himself for helplessness, with the beast for dumb subservience and paucity of ideas, with the sleeping citizens for sleeping and leaving no brightly arrowed signs to show a stranger the fastest, straightest way to quit their town, so he sped howling, barking, exploding through their neighborhoods, backing, filling, fretting in their driveways, waking the whole town to his unhappiness. By the time he chanced upon yesterday morning's highway to the north he was so incensed that he took it south, inflicting one more punishment on himself, and had to

turn around and roar north with radios blaring front
and back, but caught himself in time to turn around
toward town again at the usual place, at the foot of
those pimply hills. There would be no gas on the other
side of them, and he needed that. Besides, if he were to
leave for Oklahoma City now, without delay, he would
be there in the morning. This he could not allow himself to do, for he remembered the look of it.

He needed a drink, but did not want one if it meant,
and it did, slinking into a glass store or bar. He could
have slept, but not without that drink. The thought of
food disgusted him. Perhaps he would have watched a
movie if they would have thrown it up against the sky
where he wouldn't have to sit up to watch. Most of
the lights were still on when he arrived in town, but
the one pedestrian was Marilyn: tonight she looked a
little too plump for him, he hadn't known that her legs
were large. There were three or four cars, and the moving one honked at Claude. Claude was in his way. He
pulled to the curb to make room, and think, Big Man
sailed honking by. "Hey, sell many new homes today?"
Claude called, continuing on. A block or two later he
stopped again. But he finally stopped at Pascua, got
out this time. The Ceremony was over. In the moonlight
a few shadows were moving, talking, laughing quietly,
drinking pop, collecting the empty bottles and paper
cups in battered washtubs, sweeping dusty paths, rak-
ing cigarette butts and flowers onto Judas's smoldering
pyre.

"Hey man, sir, you want another pop?"

"Thanks, not tonight. I'm looking for a friend of
mine. Do you know Pete?" The girl stared at him. "You
don't know Pete?" he asked. She stared at the hand he
raised high above his head, but behind her a little boy's
eyes lit up. "You know big Pete, don't you, kid?"

"Yes."

"Do you know where he is?"

"They took him away again yesterday."

"Yesterday. Did they take him to the Tucson jail?"

"They took him down home again. They don't want him here."

"Hey, I guess I'll take that pop," Claude said. He gave it to the boy, who ran off with it. Then Claude left too.

"Hey, sir." It was the girl. "Are you a friend of Pedro's?"

"Yes," Claude told her. "I helped him get those flowers they threw at him." She stared. "They did throw them at him, didn't they?"

"Who," she said.

He drove to the police station to make sure what the boy had said was right. He was right in every detail, the facts were on the blotter, bellicosity confirmed the rest, and Claude soon found himself answering a rash of questions with a drawled, "Wall, Pete's a friend a mine," and scratching his country chin. But he drove south at city speed (MRS WHITES had filled No. 5 again!) and stopped at the very edge of dark to fill his tank before taking off. He had his lane all to himself tonight, but even so he was tempted to duck onto Vivien's private route—at the last minute decided not to trust himself. From there it took him less than half an hour to pass Perhaps. He knew it by a cluster of antennaed trailers around a post office-gas station named Perhaps Again. One mile to the west the Copper Castle Arms was dark, but the church and the drugbar were both ablaze. Now he was alone with his radios, getting static from the north he switched to the Nogales beam, with the help of a brisk tailwind reached the border at one o'clock. The sleepy guard was mildly surprised at sight of him, he had expected Claude earlier. Turning off a radio Claude handed his entire wallet out, his A-I Drive-away card on top. "Can you tell me where the police station is?"

"This car doesn't belong to you?"

"No, it belongs to a lady in Oklahoma City. I'm delivering it for A-I Drive-away—just as soon as I get done down here. Can you tell me how to get to the police station?"

"Do you intend to stay in Mexico long?"

"Just long enough to see a friend."

The officer returned Claude's wallet, with the card tucked in. He stepped back a step, giving him a chance to make a break for it.

"Officer, how do I get to the Nogales Police Station from here?"

"Keep straight on this road till your second left, then keep on to your second right. If you get lost, ask anyone."

"Thanks." The road kept on straight for two hundred yards or so and then bore right, Claude bearing with it through the city's thumping, bleeding heart, then left along a bleeding artery, glancing into each dark vein he passed wondering if it was perhaps wide enough to admit the beast, and stopped finally at the extremity to look for anyone. "Hey, can you tell me where the police station is?"

"Sure, sir, follow me." The boy in the fluorescent shirt lept onto the fender in front of him and waved him forward with irresistible authority, into the country a mile or two, then back again, by country roads, to the extremities, here waved them plunging into the city again, urging, cajoling, shaming Claude into dark alleys that somehow sucked in their urinary walls just in time to avoid the beast's uneasy flanks, even when she had to turn, as she so often did, but at last into the heart again, failing now, and onto that same artery, hardening, dark, where his guide waved Claude two-armed to a stop. "Right here," he said, and he was right. Claude turned off the motor and the radios, gave the boy a dime to get him off the door.

"Hey sir, I watch your caps for you."

"No thanks."

"O.K. I watch them for you."

"No."

"O.K., sir. . . ."

"You get home to bed. I'll be a long time in here."

"O.K., I don't have school till nine."

"I guess you'd better watch them then."

"O.K., sir."

Music, it was the indefatigable song Claude had just turned off, seeped from the station into the street. Behind the glass door a pair of officers draped on wooden armchairs decorating a smoky room, each man's legs extending to the arm of the other's chair, ankles nicely crossed, stomachs bulging tight khaki shirts, but shoulders very wide and sharp above big black-holstered guns. They were listening to a pigskin portable radio on a shelf above their heads. As the door opened one swung his fancy boots onto the floor in front of him, decided not to stand in them. Claude found it hard to look up in time to smile into the waiting eyes, but possible. Closing the door he shouted "Goodmorning" politely too.

"What can we do for you, sir?"

"I guess I'm a little early or late," Claude said, and smiled again, "but I hear you're holding a man named Pedro Martin here. The Tucson police said they brought him down on Saturday."

"What's the name of that man?" asked the cop with his boots on the floor.

"Pedro Martin."

"Pedro Martinez," interpreted the reclining cop. They discussed briefly between themselves, and then he asked, "What is it you want, sir?"

"Is Pedro Martinez here?"

"You mean Pedro Martinez, you mean that Indian?"

"Yes."

"You mean that wetback Indian?" asked the seated cop.

"Yes."

They discussed again, while the reclining cop lit a fresh cigarette with the other cop's. "Sir, what do you want him for?" asked the reclining cop.

"Well, I want to help him if I can."

They laughed. Claude didn't, so they laughed again for him. "You can help that Indian," said the seated cop. "You can dig a hole for him."

"A big one," said the reclining cop, spreading his muscular arms.

"We don't want to," the other said, coughing, his shoulders sagging toward his boots, and when Claude smiled at him: "What can we do for you, sir?"

"Can I see him?"

Smiling, smoking, they shook their heads. "It's too late to go in there now. It's late, sir. Everyone is asleep in there."

"I'll wait until morning then."

"All right, sir. What would you like, sir?" one asked, for Claude was looking around the room.

"I was wondering if there's some place I could shave."

"Shave? Certainly right in there, sir."

"Thanks. I'll get my bag."

It was dark outside, the moon was gone. Claude gasped the cool air cautiously, coughed up smoke. In the car the luminous boy lay on his back, smoking and listening to radio.

"I watch your caps, sir!"

Claude passed a nickel in to him. "I'll be right back."

In the station the cops glanced only briefly at his imitation leather bag. "Right in there, sir." This washroom could have used some smoke, but Claude had left all his outside. He shaved his hostile beard as quickly as he could, and afterwards he put on his tie. When he stepped out the door the energetic cop got to his boots, but not the other one. "Do you want to wait here for the chief, sir?" asked the upright cop, waving to his chair. "I'm off duty now. You can listen to the radio."

"What time does the chief come in?"

"About eight or ten."

"Thanks, I guess I'll get some sleep and come back then."

"All right, sir."

Outside he wished he had not bared his face, the wind was cool. The boy had fallen asleep, and Claude stood at the door jingling coins until he woke up. "Sir . . ."

"Thanks very much," Claude said, handing him a dime as he climbed out. "That's all for tonight."

"Will you come back?"

"Not tonight."

The boy closed Claude's door for him, whacked his fender as it passed by. "O.K., sir," he called, and Claude called thanks, but in his mirrors he could see the glowing shirt already streaking into an alley across the street. He drove out along the main artery as far as the boy had taken him, to a racetrack there, parked the beast beneath a palm tree in the parking lot. Before lying down he locked the doors, took off his shoes, turned off the radio. Even with all the windows closed it was a chilly night, but his squire had thought to warm his bed for him.

He awoke in daylight, to a low persistent slapping just outside his door, just behind his head, like a child firming pies or castles in damp sand. Yet this seemed unlikely, for he remembered parking on macadam the night before, and through the windshield he could see what appeared to be his same palm tree standing there. He lay absolutely still, wide open, listening, trying to make this out. Was some one stripping his caps, planting dynamite, or what? He could not decide. Slowly he raised himself on one stiff elbow, craned his head on his stiff neck: as his eyes reached window level, the slapping stopped. An old grey animal it was. He lay on the macadam a few feet off, long-haired, long-legged, long-tailed, long-faced, almost a dog, not quite. Too lean, too cynical. He had stiffened all over at sight of Claude, but now under Claude's stare he turned his head to look cynically at some distant point, squeal like a pup, relax his tail and slap again. Claude turned on the radio. He could not make out the words, but the tone sounded like the seven o'clock news if anything. He switched it off, saw the coyote still waiting there. Putting on his shoes, unlocking and pushing the door, he said, "Hi, boy," softly as he slid slowly out. The coyote lay tensely watching him. "Nice fellow," Claude said, and the coyote began slapping hard. Claude patted the cool nose he offered up, and the coyote followed him around the beast while he checked her caps. He was quite a coyote; Claude stood for a minute at the door admiring him. "Well, so long, boy," he said getting in, waiting for the nose to draw away from the closing door. He patted the quivering nose and the delighted coyote climbed in on him. "No, boy. No!" The coyote backed squealing out, the entire rear half of him wagging now, his head nodding fervently to the right. He wanted to get in the back. "Sorry, boy," Claude said, and slammed the door. The coyote ran beside the door across the parking lot, along the road with him for a block or so, but when Claude speeded up he stopped. Claude slowed down. He could see the coyote standing in the middle of the road, watching after him until he was out of sight. If the coyote had begun to run again, he told himself, he would have stopped to wait for him. Since the coyote had not, he hurried off. In town he treated himself to a caustic omelette before he went to see the chief.

This morning an empty police car was parked tail-first in front of the station door, with motor running, emitting from both ends a stinking steam. The station door was blind with steam, but inside some of the smoke had cleared. Last night's reclining policeman was yawning on his feet, the chief was seated behind a coffin-desk. Slight-chinned but mustachioed, he drank his coffee rather testily, yet answered Claude's goodmorning with a charming smile. Drinking he listened closely to what the policeman had to say to him, nodded when he was through, and looked up to smile at Claude again. "Sir, what can we do for you?" Now he listened with thoughtfully tucked-in chin to every word that Claude and the policeman said, nodded when they both were through. "Sir," he said. and frowned at Claude, "this man's crime is making illegal entrance into the United States. This is the fourteenth time he's done this thing." He shrugged. "This man is chronic, sir. We don't want this man. This man is a trouble and an expense to us. We're sick of him. The best thing to do with him is put him in jail for life imprisonment." Again he shrugged. "We can't do that—he eats too much. So we keep him here for thirty days and then he goes back again. In this way the Sonora Government and the United States Government share this man's expense. We don't want him, sir. Nobody wants this man. Everyone is sick of him. If this man would pay his fine we would let him out."

"How much is his fine?"

"If he would pay his fine we would let him out," the chief said, but shrugged. "He won't pay. He says he doesn't have any money left from all his work up there. So we keep him here for thirty days and then he goes back again."

"How much would it take to get him out?"

The chief looked at Claude, and then he looked at his empty coffee cup. "Fifty dollars." He set the cup aside. "United States."

Claude had two bonds left, a fifty and a twentyfive, both immature. The chief took them from Claude's hand, spread them out on his desk to study them. Soon, without looking up, he returned the twenty-five to Claude.

"No, these haven't reached face value yet," Claude told him. "You'll need them both."

"Ah. Ah." The chief took back the twentyfive. "You can cash these at the bank," he said, folding them, tucking them in his pocket. "I'll show you where."

He looked once more at his coffee cup before he rose. He got his hat. Carefully adjusting its peak, almost straight, not quite, he spoke a few words to the cop. Now he escorted Claude across the room, held the door for him. He held the car door too, and when Claude was in he slammed it hard for him against the acrid smoke. Slamming his own door, he delicately pressed in the hand throttle, stomping meanwhile with his foot until he had caught the choking motor up. He turned on his windshield wiper, the only one, and while he waited for it to do its work he wiped steam from both their windows with his sleeve. "It's very wet today," he said as they lurched off.

They sped through a narrow alley, around the block, parked aslant before the bank. The chief turned his ignition off, quickly on again. Too late. Glancing at one another, they got out and slammed their doors. The bank wasn't open yet, but when the chief rapped his rings against the glass a pretty girl ran forward. When he smiled some charming steam at her, she ran off. The chief smiled at his reflection in the glass. "She'll be right back," he said. She was. Opening the door a crack for them, she blushed goodmorning at the sidling chief, smiled a pretty smile for Claude. They followed her to her window, where the chief spoke to her earnestly at length. She listened to every work he said, then took the bonds he held to her and studied them. He spoke earnestly again, so she held a pen to Claude. The chief showed him where to write. Now the girl began to count the money out, but the chief asked her for United States. Slowly, in full sight upon the counter, he meted out the dollars in two separate piles, $50 for himself, $8.75 for Claude. "Sí," he said, squaring the edges of his pile, pushing Claude's to him. He and the girl chatted gaily as she walked with him to the door, opened it a little, quickly closed it after them.

The chief stepped briskly across the street. "It's wet," he said. "We can walk." On the way he pointed out several buildings, people, cars, spoke of the city's progressiveness, his department's progressiveness. "It's not usually this wet," he said, holding the door for Claude. He spoke shortly to the reclining cop, who left the room at once. The chief hung up his hat. Seated at his desk, he made out a beautiful receipt and handed it to Claude, pulled out another paper which he placed beside his coffee cup. While they waited he took it up and read it over to himself.

"Pete."

Pete still had his puttees on, ancient cracking leather puttees laced to his bursting calves with bits of string, making slack blue jodhpurs of his jeans. He still wore an old khaki shirt over his blue shirt, spotted where it wasn't bleached, bagging from his belly to his belt but popping buttons at his chest. "Hi, mister," he called to Claude. The chief handed him his paper and Pete folded it, slipped it inside his shirts. The chief waved him to the cop, who led Pete to another desk. Opening the right-hand bottom drawer the cop passed him his visored chauffeur's cap, his tin sheriff's star, and, after a brief debate with the chief, his wooden gun. Everyone waited while Pete put on his hat, pinned on his star, tucked his gun handily at his waist. Then both the chief and the cop stood up, ushered Pete and Claude across the room. At the door, the chief shook hands with Claude. He patted Pete. "Good luck," he called, and they looked back through the door, no longer fogged, to answer his wave, his charming smile. For appearance sake, they turned the beast around and headed south. When they were past the station, Pete laughed and held out his hand. "Hey, you got me out."

Laughing too, Claude shook his hand. "It was easy."

[131]

"How much does it cost?"

"Don't worry about that now."

"How much?"

"Fifty dollars."

"Hey, that's cheap. I pay you back."

"When you can."

"I pay back my fine," Pete said. "If I pay them my fine they take every dollar from my bank. I send you soon. You tell me where to send it to."

"O.K.," Claude said. "You want to go back to Watsonville?"

"I guess I do."

"Do you think you'd better ride in the trunk a while?"

"Not the trunk!" Pete said, and laughed. "In the trunk they always catch me in the patrol."

"They didn't look there when I came in."

"It's *out* you came, not in," Pete explained to him. "I show you where to turn down here."

They turned east through an adobe suburb of casually subdivided lots, tiny, queerly fenced, then sped nowhere for a few miles, now veered off between two brown fields in which herds of skinny dogs were being watched by half a dozen fretful cows. The train led directly to an old mesquite tree with well-chewed trunk and limbs which cast a finicky shade over the hapless ground beneath, barren, stained dark with sweat, crushed by who knew how many tons of animal. Claude parked a few yards away.

"It's only puddles today!" called Pete, one-legged in the groaning tree. "I can jump over them." He stepped down and they walked together part way to the wadi bank, until Pete dropped to his stomach, peered around. He glanced at Claude beside him. "You want to meet me over there?"

"Sure."

"O.K., you see that tree in U.S.A.?"

"Yes."

"O.K., you drive your car one mile past Nogales U.S.A., then you turn her right at the Hello Amigos! sign. Then you look for those little rock heaps we have there until you see that tree. You see me under it. O.K.?"

"O.K., I guess."

"I see you over there," Pete said, creeping forward on his belly. At the edge he waved before dropping out of sight, and Claude watched until he saw him down in the wadi bed, slogging puttee-deep in mud, but slogging fast. Then Claude ran back to the beast, circled the mesquite tree, hurried roundabout to U.S.A.

Pete was right about the patrol, going in. They were only mildly interested in Claude's having no license plates, but they questioned him closely about fruits and vegetables. When he declared his strawberry jam, they waved it aside and asked for the key to his trunk. They spent quite a while back there, and when they came forward they looked under his fenders too. They lifted his hood, looked all around, felt around, slammed it closed. A line of muttering cars had formed in back, and the vexed patrol waved Claude on. "All right," they said. Thanking them, he pip-pipped north. He drove that mile past Nogales U.S.A., turned right at the Hello Amigos! sign, noting the little rock heap at its base. Here a bridge of two ant-holed planks, warped and pigeon-toed, spanned a narrow southbound wadi. There were other rock heaps every quarter mile or so along the wadi, with a wide selection of tracks inter-lacing them: all led, regardless of one's taste, to that lone cottonwood. Not so lonely now with Pete squatting in its well-trampled shade. Pete waited for the car to stop before he stood up.

"Was it easy?"

"Very."

"O.K., now I try your trunk a while."

Claude opened it and Pete rolled in upon his back, resting his head in the cradle of the spare—he knew cars. "O.K., lock me up," he said, and grinned. He rapped the door when Claude had locked. "Turn on your radio."

Claude turned the back one on, circled the tree, followed those heaps out to the road. For the first time today, he relaxed. The sun was high and warm, not nearly hot, that omelette had finally worked its way down through his guts, even the raucous music began to reach him as it had not last night. The beast too seemed pleased. Stopping to fill her up at a country store, it amused him to watch the watchers suspiciously eyeing her from their bench. He smiled at the one who pumped the gas. "Nice day," he said, but the old man was working too hard to do more than grunt. He was weak and his gas was strong. Claude nodded to the other watchers, but a moment later climbed coughing out, to see who else had coughed: happily it was the pumping man. His gas was strong, and a strong blue smoke was escaping from the trunk into his face. "I guess that's enough," Claude said. Coughing, the old man hung up. Claude followed him into the store, where he made his careful change. "Thanks," Claude said on his way out, and the old man grunted behind his handkerchief. The others stared. Claude felt himself: his fly was closed, his pants stayed up. He hadn't realized he'd been away this long. He would have turned back to Mexico, Arivada, The Office, anywhere, for them, but they did not mention it. They sat on their privacy and watched the beast pip off. Claude waved goodbye, waved again for Pete.

They were somewhere between the border and Perhaps, roughly thirty miles deep in U.S.A., when they came upon their first pedestrians. Two girls, both tall, walked on the righthand side of the highway with their backs to the northbound beast. Between them hung a large brown package bound by heavy wire, with a handle at either end. Apart from the unexpected pleasure of seeing them here, what most impressed Claude was the slight, provocative bias of their necks. Had there been only one of them he might not have noticed anything, for this was not a deformity. It was nonetheless a tendency, forward and to the right, which began down by their blue T-shirts until it emerged in those pale drooping necks from which head and hair hung forward mostly out of sight. Yet there was no sloth, no slipshod, in their gait. If anything they trod ground with an uncommon vigor, as though breaking it. And when at the last instant they turned to confront the startled beast, they did not have to free their outside hands from their hip pockets nor unpackage their inside ones to make Claude slow down, nor smile to make him stop.

"What is it again, the patrol?" called Pete.

"No. Girls."

"What girls?" Pete thumped the trunk.

"Let's wait and see," Claude hissed, tuning the backseat radio up. He smiled through the window at the slouching girls, who smiled back prettily. Now they did lift their thumbs in vague solicitation, waiting for the door to swing. Claude slapped red leatherette: "Hello. Hop in!"

"Thanks." They slid. But seated they were altogether presentable, almost trim, their long black hair concealed their curvatures. Their similar faces were delicate, lovely things, in which teeth seemed rather large and out of place. Their package was sent via air mail, SPECIAL DELIVERY. "Very nice of you to stop."

"How far are you going?"

"Just around this bend." They showed him where to turn, left, onto a rocky road which he hit much too hard by way of pardoning loud new thumps inside the trunk, only making things that much worse. "Loose spare," he apologized, dialing another radio.

"This isn't a very nice road," one said.

"You live out here?"

"Yes, just over there. You can see our smoke."

He could indeed, a fine white smoke seeping from what appeared to be an ancient moving van, very long, almost as high, once blue but piebald now. Beyond, a lower, rambling structure, of corrugated iron intermeddled with boards and rocks, issued its own thin smoke. Otherwise there was no visible activity, all doors were shut, all gaps and windows plugged, but all around and in between a tremendous wash sagged from wires and palo verde trees. At least a dozen pair of jeans, three times that many underpants, and the other things proportionately.

"You seem to have a good-sized family."

"Yes." They pointed out the driveway, a skinny one forged long ago by that once-moving van. "You can turn in here." Now the scratch of palo verde thorns against howling paint distracted even Claude's attention from the thumping trunk. He followed the would-be drive as far as he could, just short of where the van had for no clear reason stopped. Perhaps it had run out of gas, or more likely one of its dainty tires had sprung a leak, you could not say with certainty because the whole thing hung just off the ground on piles of rocks. And a wire ran to the roof from a nearby power pole, dismissing all thought of gas.

"Is this all right?"

"Just fine," they said.

Since the girls made no move to leave the car at once, Claude sat waiting too, listening with them to some sort of preparatory movement inside the van. But his curiosity had faltered sidewise to the girls by the time the big back doors broke suddenly open, thus he caught the scene with only the dim fringes of his sight, as: a tall human figure materializing from a flash of brilliant albino light. This deception, no doubt fortuitous, was reasonably explained by a moon-size bulb above the tall man's head and improved by his pure white beard and white coveralls. Too, not a muscle in this gaunt apparition twitched. The girls slid from the car, Claude out his side, all three of them (and Pete?) at disheveled attention like the stunned crew of a fire engine being inspected by the Secretary of Defense. His old eyes were first to waver, from the beast to Claude, to the girls or the ground beneath. "Yes, Ionia?"

"Dad, we've brought a visitor."

His eyes flicked over the beast, away. "Where from, Latvia?"

Pointing out Claude's windshield sticker Latvia said, "Dad, Oklahoma, U.S. of A."

At that he quickly raised his eyes, looked down at Claude quite pleasantly. He smiled. "Welcome, partner," he said, spreading his arms outside the van. "You're the first I've met from there. Do you know the Choctaw well?" He bent gracefully at the waist to extend beautiful hands toward Claude. "St. Jones," he said.

"Squires. Claude Squires," Claude said, taking the bony hands, being taken in by them.

"Squires? That's aphetic, isn't it, and in a sense epithetic too. A fine young name. But come, let's not stand out here in the strontium. Will you step inside and sign the register?" He drew back and Claude climbed up to him, the girls closely following. When they were all inside, Mr. St. Jones swung the doors. It was like waking up, they all stood squinting painfully in the excessive light, Claude of course the least prepared. His 20-10 vision was of little help to him. When at last he had his eyes under partial control, he found a large woman in very tight black jeans and T-shirt studying him suspiciously from her cast iron stove, or at least uncertainly. Perhaps she had already smiled hello, was vexed with him. Mr. St. Jones cleared his throat and took up the register, flipped pages to the U.S. of A., indicated with his pen where he wanted Claude to sign.

He had it arranged by states, a line for each, perhaps three quarters of them filled. Oregon and Ohio were accounted for, New York, New Jersey, Nevada, Florida, all the C's, Arizona of course, but not Arkansas. Alaska though. Claude gave his full name, his age, sex, height and, under Mr. St. Jones's close monitorship, his true weight. Mr. St. Jones retrieving the register appeared greatly pleased, nodded his beard several times before closing up. "Ah, a skinny one, a fine young ectomorph? Sit down there, partner."

"Thank you." He sat where he could, on the low couch or bed, beside a very high easel with a fresh painting on it. The intensely colored picture was of two plump pink lovers leaning across an antique sun dial for a kiss. Their shadow fell over the face of the dial, obliterating time, but a Geiger counter lay madly ticking there. Other Geigers, one hanging by a strap from the back of the plump man's belt, the other a pendant at his girl-friend's neck, ticked as well. The blithe lovers smiled.

"I paint," Mr. St. Jones apologized, from a lofty height.

"Yes, I see." Claude studied other paintings on the walls, similar scenes, people, themes, a plump master of the barbecue stooping for a Pioneer potato chip that promised to burn a hole in him, a plump cur furtively burying a juicy radioactive bone, a plump horse, etc.

"Not seriously anymore since the war began," said Mr. St. Jones, "only for sustenance. I merely illustrate. Yet my daubs may repay a moment's study, there's more to them than immediately meets the eye. For example, those protuberances there," he said, with a long brush tracing the substantial buttocks of the amorous man, "they aren't what they seem to be. Not just twin hoards of quivering blubber, the common encumbrances of an idle life. No, those are tumors," he said. "And also those:" his brush outlined the young lady's bust. "Publishers alway edit my rearends," he said, "however, not my chests. They expunge my counters too of course. Yet I continue to put them in, always hoping that one will slip through someday." He paused to smile down at Claude with his calm old eyes. "We can hope, can't we," he said.

"We certainly can."

Mr. St. Jones's eyes glistened behind a halo of lashes, his voice fell soft and husky, as if with love. "Did you say you know the Choctaw well?"

"No, I . . . "

Mr. St. Jones smiled and nodded his encouragement, for he was much pleased. "We must get word to them," he agreed, extending his brush to a painting on the wall —a tumorous sportsman luring tumorous fish with a barbed and wildly ticking one. "That picture appeared in the March 15 *Outdoor Sport*, illustrating a story entitled "Meet Mr. Crappie!" on page 21. *Outdoor Sport* has a paid circulation of 1,000,078, plus the libraries, hospitals, and barbershops—imagine the possibilities if one of my counters had got through, even with most of my tumors removed. Sensational! A leak like that could curtail the war by as much as ten to twenty years, or more. . . . But I don't imagine many Choctaw subscribe to *Outdoor Sport*?"

"One did leak through, partially, Dad," said one of the girls. "In the December *True or False*."

"That's right, Latvia." Mr. St. Jones's voice was husky with the same strong emotion he had earlier shown toward Claude. "That's right."

Ionia said, "They left just enough that you could tell what it was."

"That's right, Ionia," murmured Mr. St. Jones, turning to a painting above Claude's head. "Notice where I've placed the counter in this one, partner"—between the legs of a widely known movie star, tumorously enhanced, floating voluptuously downstream on an innertube. "You can see their predicament—they had to leave something there. They left about half of it, like so, enough for any normally perceptive man to make it out. Incidentally, this picture has been submitted to *Libel* too—she paid me to do it herself, but that's neither here nor there," he said as the lights went out.

There was a breathless quiet inside the van, and of course a spectacular dark. "Don't worry, it's just the Yellow Trucks," Mr. St. Jones whispered over Claude, "out wondering where all their power's going. Willie has disconnected our extension cord until they give up. It won't take long. Poor devils, they don't know what to make of it, 500,000 kilowatts a day unaccounted for. I understand they're building a great new dam up north," he said, the girls tittering softly in the dark. "More power to them," he admonished. "We'll need that too before very long. Have you visited it yet, the dam?"

"No, not . . ."

"A big one, ay?" he whispered, and Claude could imagine him nodding his beard enthusiastically. "Well, let's hope they get it done in time, hey, partner? We can hope," he said.

"We can."

The light flared on.

"All clear!" Mr. St. Jones announced, smiling and straightening his straight back. "Willie has reconnected us. That didn't take long, now did it, partner? A man could almost feel pity for the Yellow Trucks, if he forgot for a moment his history. I'd like to show you our layout, if you care to step next door? Girls. We'll be back in a few minutes, Joy," he said, and the black-jeaned woman slunk back to her cast iron range. Mr. St. Jones took Claude's arm.

"Dad, you forgot your mail," Latvia and Ionia said.

"Excuse me. Thank you for reminding me, girls, thank you for delivering it too. My publishers pay off only once a week so it's quite an event for us, isn't it, girls?" he apologized as he took the package from Latvia and Ionia. Smiling shyly at Claude, they flexed the fingers of their inside hands. "Here are your handles, girls, and wire. Here's your paper, Joy," he called, and Joy came after it. "Don't forget to take the labels off," and Joy returned muttering to her range. Claude saw her stuff the wrapping into the fire, SPECIAL DELIVERY labels and all, but the family was too engrossed with the mail to take heed, or care. Claude too before very long. At a glance from Mr. St. Jones he tucked his feet beneath the bed so that the topmost layer, the candles, stationery, pencils, toilet tissue, turpentine and postage stamps could be spread out for all to see upon the floor. This was only the frosting though. Here came the jeans, the T-shirts, the underpants, the fuses and radio tubes, the electric cord and bulbs, and wrapped inside the white coveralls a bottle of cognac which Mr. St. Jones examined carefully before gently shoving it beneath the bed. "Prewar," he said. "Produced and bottled in 1943, stored ever since in an airtight cave near Cannes. Latvia, I'm afraid they forgot your diaphram—but they remembered the diapers, happily. Here's Bill and Buck and John and Tom and Henry's razorblades." He passed the diapers and blades over his head to her. "Ionia, here's your bubblegum—remember now, only five minutes per day. And here's Willie's too." He handed it back to her. "Here are your matches, Joy," but Joy did not come immediately after them. She waited until Mr. St. Jones had placed them on the floor, then she snatched them up. "Partner, I'm afraid there's not a thing for you. Unless you'd like some razorblades?"

"No, no thanks . . . "

"Ionia, give our guest a bubblegum."

Ionia did as she was told, she even peeled his paper off. She read the cartoon to herself before passing it. When Claude had read it too, she passed his gum. Seeing him hesitate, she blew a little bubble at him. Chewing he directed his blushing attention to the wall again.

"That's about it," Mr. St. Jones was saying, peering inside the box. "Except of course my canvases. Ho, what's this, a note.'Sorry we couldn't send the diaphram —we're ordering from Los Angeles. Yrs, Ray,'" he read, and looked up at tittering Latvia. "Latvia . . ." He dropped the note back in the box, closed the flaps, shoved the box behind the bed. "Shall we step next door, partner?" he asked, erecting rather stiffly on his legs. "Ionia, your five minutes is up," he snapped, and "Joy, we'll be right back!" He swung the doors and they hurried out, Latvia first, Ionia and Claude, then Mr. St. Jones, who slammed and bolted when they were clear. A counter hung upside down above the door, rat-a-tat-tatting ominously, almost drowning out the thumps from within the trunk, Claude hadn't noticed this before. He was starting toward the car with the thought of freeing Pete, who might pass for Choctaw here, but Mr. St. Jones was beckoning urgently.

"Getting heavier every day, hey, partner?" he called, turning up the collar of his coveralls, ducking his head as he ran before them to the corrugated house. "That's the real thing there, pre-war," he called, pointing back to the rat-tat-tat. "Never inspected by the government. You knew they've been putting governors on them since declaring war in '45, and mufflers too? Don't forget to tell the Choctaw that." He held his collar tight with one hand and with the other held the door. "The girls paint too," he said, but just then Ionia took Claude's near arm, high up beneath the pit. Claude threw his gum away before entering.

The corrugated house, one large haphazard cavity, was savagely alight with several moon-size bulbs that hung from cords far too long for this low room, so that one faced everywhere a choice between slink and scorch. Perhaps that was how the girls had won their necks. Or perhaps by arching critically, as they did now, from and toward the canvases which Mr. St. Jones referred to with a paintbrush that was long and slightly bowed:

for the most part interiors, or undergrounds, of pocked and craggy holes, rock vaults with mossy floors and slimy walls, or narrow scenic vistas that skinny silver streams squirmed through like sidewinders flipped on their backs, beneath downward grasping tentacles of roots, stalactites dagger-sharp and dangling by threads of stone, stalagmites teetering, all doused, frozen in molten electric white that suggested what a glimpse of hell might be, too beautiful, some still lifes too, great bulbous beets, hoary legumes, giant scallions, white carrots, tomatoes, berries, squash in huge radiant bowls, and portraits, signed by Ionia, of shadows, from which gleamed eyes and teeth and nails and, here and there, a glowing bubble, or scrotum, caught the eye. Near the door a counter clacked but rather quietly. Otherwise the room was bare except for five or six men squatting in the corners, mixing paints.

"Well, partner, do you begin to see the light?" asked
"Yes!"

"Cavism is tomorrow's art," murmured Mr. St. Jones, discarding the brush to render cavism full emotion of look and voice. "Who can say how long it will take the rest of us to grow up to it? I suppose we'll cling for a generation or two to the old nostalgic scenes and ways, the sun and the moon and the barbecue? Hasn't it always been so, even among the Choctaw? I'll admit to occasional lapses of the kind myself when one of the girls brings a fresh work to me, a quiver of something like disgust and, in Ionia's case, even shock. But the day will come when we'll be able to open our eyes and see the new world in all its beauty, in its natural light, unobstructed by dawn and dusk, in all its pristine purity, uncontaminated by strontium and sin. When that day comes, my Latvia and my Ionia will be recognized for what they are, mothers of the new world art, at least of its early objective-representational phase."

"It's what . . . ?" But Ionia had grasped Claude high

up under the pit again and was leading him to her portraiture. "That's my Willie," she said, with a nod of her neck. "That's Latvia's Bill . . . Her Buck . . . I think that's her Tom . . ."

"Ionia," Latvia cried, "do you have to tell everyone *everything* . . . ?"

"That's her Henry," Ionia whispered with a small sidewise nod, and showing teeth.

"Ionia, come here!" Mr. St. Jones stood waiting for her to approach, with Claude. Then, "I apologize for raising my voice to you, Ionia," he said, "but darling. . . . " He turned briefly to Latvia and then to the stirring boys, called: "How's it going there, partners?"

"Just fine, Saint Jones," they said.

"Latvia has your razorblades."

"Thanks, Saint Jones."

"Well, partner," he said, taking Claude's free arm, "now that you've seen our layout here, would you care to step downstairs?"

"Sir?"

"We'll be right back, boys."

"All right, Saint Jones."

Saint Jones and Claude watched Latvia and Ionia roll back the rug, lift a trap door and hold it high.

"Partner? After you."

"All right, Saint Jones."

At least a hundred steps, to be taken backward in newish shoes, with Ionia toddling lightly on his hands above, since Latvia was mashing hers, and Saint Jones urging him all the while, "Latvia? Ionia? What's the trouble, girls?" Then at half-mast forward along a corridor gnawed long ago by a single-minded midget who had not had Ionia clinging to his beltless hips while dealing uppercuts to Latvia with her heels, or butting him softly between the legs whenever Latvia struck back or bit or pinched or Saint Jones called, "Partner? Everything all right down there?" "Just fine, Saint

Jones, just fine," he called and called, and plunged at last into a room which would have demented the Yellow Trucks and maybe the Choctaw too, a room illumed by at least a dozen chandeliers, a livingroom, with sofas, chairs, footstools, reading lamps, family portraits on the walls.

"Sit down a minute, partner," urged Saint Jones. "Don't rush off until you've visited awhile."

But on the other hand Ionia had caught Claude up and was leading him to a large gilt-framed oil above the mantelpiece (which decorated a crackling electric fire) and whispering loudly in his ear: "That's Latvia."

"Ah." He had seen it, upstairs, in miniature, as a pocked and craggy cave, an interior.

"Ionia!" Saint Jones grasped Claude's other arm, drawing him aside. "Sit down on the daveno, partner, by the fire," he said, and Claude obeyed. Latvia and Ionia sat opposite him on a matching daveno, while Saint Jones stood stiff before the mantelpiece, his bony hands warming behind his back, his noble white head partially concealing Ionia's likeness of Latvia. "This room here," Saint Jones began, "is about all that remains of the original house. It dates back some sixty-five or seventy years, to the first groundwork laid by two brothers with the name of Snell. It's been enlarged and remodeled several times since by various occupants, new rooms have been added, others have been torn down or have fallen in. The property was occupied continuously for fifty-odd years, until the lead-zinc market took a dive soon after the war began. There's no uranium or plutonium or thorium at all down here"—Saint Jones indicated a counter lying on the mantelpiece, paralyzed—"so the poor blind fools abandoned it. I happened upon it soon afterward, in '46, while fleeing from the Bikini blast. What a depths-sent blessing that I misread my evacuation map! I staked claim at once, and we've been here ever since, improving, exploring, enlarging, as much as time permits. We spend virtually all our after-noons down here. Whenever the bombs are falling we stay down here around the clock, with rotating two-hour shifts topside to look out for the Yellow Trucks. But during lulls like the present one our working hours are spent mostly topside, for appearance sake. Naturally we look forward to the day when appearances will be reversed, when to venture onto the ground—or, what's worse, off of it—will be the mark of an anti-social crank, a suicidal maniac. That day isn't as far off as some may think," he said, adding with lowered voice, "We are promised this on good authority from below. We expect to be entirely self-sufficient when that time comes. In fact we are already, to a great extent. We still get our mail, of course, but that will pass. We grow all our own vegetables and fruits—I'll show you our garden soon. Latvia is learning to make some first-rate jeans and coveralls, with moss. We're hoarding our lightbulbs constantly, and in the near future we plan a full-scale raid on the Yellow Trucks. We won't need razorblades. All partners will be permitted to grow beards, until the facial hair dies out. Aren't the Choctaw relatively beardless, like the Chickasaw? For canvases we'll use my publishers' mailing boxes, until Latvia perfects her method for laminating moss—I myself will retire, of course. Excellent bristles can be made with beard. We make all our own paints of lead and zinc, as you've seen," he said. "Ionia will do without her bubblegum. Shall we step into the garden now?"

"By all means, Saint Jones."

Saint Jones led the way back across the livingroom and down an opposite corridor, a higher, more modern one, enlivened with interiors. "This is the master bed-room," he explained, pausing at a large, spotlessly tidy room luxuriantly appointed in white decor. "And this Latvia's," he said of a room almost as large but barely furnished with a sewing machine and a great rock-to-rock moss rug. "Here's Ionia's"—a cubbyhole. "We haven't found need for a guest room yet, but the day may come. The garden is straight ahead outdoors."

Ionia secured Claude's arm and they entered an outdoors that put the topside sun to shame, a lush half-acre of exquisitely cultivated garden in which basked vegetables and fruits identical to those in Latvia's still lifes—beets, sprouts, onions, scallions, pears, legumes, each one true to kind though colorless and swelling horribly before the eyes. In their midst brooded a tattered effigy, fat and tightly blackjeaned along the lines of Joy, for scaring bats. Saint Jones bent to pluck a weed of the nettle class, he could have punctured a Yellow Truck. "Our garden is still in the experimental stage," he said, "but it seems to be doing quite well. Latvia, didn't Joy mention having corn for lunch?"

"All right, Dad." Latvia chose an ear and Ionia gave up Claude long enough to help her carry it indoors.

"Our garden has sustained us for almost five years," Saint Jones continued, "for the past three exclusively. We eat little meat. Bat stew is tolerable, if you go heavy on the vegetables. But in the main our diet is a meatfree one. I think it's done a world of good for all of us. Show our partner your figures, girls." Palely blushing, the girls tossed back their hair: it was true, their chests were absolutely tumorless. "Hard to believe they belong to the Radioactive Generation, partner, eh? I'm sure we get all our vitamins and minerals, plus a few not found above. The same can be said for calories. Try a scallion if you wish, they're particularly good this year. You've had your lunch? Then take one for the road—I know the Choctaw will be interested. A word of caution: thus far our garden is necessarily limited to our own needs. What surplus we have is marketed by our California partner, man by the name of Saki, who reports great success. Shall we visit the temple next? Straight down that path ahead. What is that, west?"

[147]

Claude could not say. He followed Ionia down a sloping path, past familiar cavist scenes, deep craggy holes with oozing walls, squirming streams, stalagmites precariously erect, rude hanging and dripping things. Here again the girls had allowed themselves the artist's one violation of truth, they had made it bearable. Claude looked once more at Latvia, thought he saw her blush. Ionia caught it too. "Poor Latvia . . ."

"Shall we all take off our shoes and socks," Saint Jones said.

They all did and this time he went first, into a vault almost as bright as the outdoors itself, what with the indirect lighting from the floor, the generous candelabra that flanked either side of the altar, the great incandescent altarpiece (⚭ TO ⚮) plus the many devotional bulbs flickering in recesses along the walls. The room otherwise was as bare as Latvia's—even more, the floor had been shorn of moss, so that walking stimulated seductively the tender undersoles. Yet it seemed there was more here than met the downcast eye. "Do you see that writing on the wall," asked Saint Jones after twice rising on his toes and arching his head backwards, as did the girls, most gracefully, "it dates back some six hundred years to the year of our partner 26 a.p." That old emotion again, many times multiplied: "Of humble birth, he taught himself to write at twentyfive. I came upon it quite by accident, while hunting moss for Latvia. The profoundest story ever told, all right here in lead and zinc." Claude could see it now, roughly scratched, or delicately clawed by hammer, upon the walls. "I'm copying and translating it," murmured Saint Jones. "I've got this far—his hand swept midway up on the righthand wall. "Have you often wondered what became of the pre-Pueblo cliff dwellers when they abandoned the cliffs some six or seven hundred years ago? They're there," and he lowered his eyes ecstatically to the floor. "Yes, it's all recorded here, the word of cliff.

They're working day and night below, building a great new land for all of us, red, yellow, brown, black and white alike. When everything has been prepared, our partner will ascend from underneath and lead us to the promised place.''

"When is he coming, Dad?"

"Latvia and Ionia, I haven't got that far. Meanwhile I'm translating just as fast as I can, and digging too. I've communicated with him, by hammertap. However, he usually speaks to me only of particularities, such as my rate of progress, the condition of my hammer and pick, which way to go. He speaks very highly of the Choctaw,'' Saint Jones said aside to Claude, and then went on: "With the guidance of our partner I'm undertaking a vast worldround network of interconnecting corridors for him to lead us down to safety on that promised day. There's excellent country around the Alabaster Caverns,'' Saint Jones gravely reminded Claude, quoting cliff, ''and all through the panhandle area. I'm told bicycles will be provided for the trip. Beyond that I don't know much beyond the year 26 a.p., or to be more exact 133 b.c., which is where I am now in the book. I don't even know with any surety what our partner looks like, outwardly, no pictures or images are extant. I do know that he's an extraordinarily large and powerful man, he had to be in order to climb all the way up here to leave his book. I assume he still has his hair and red pigmentation, though he promises us that in time we'll all be bald and grey. The book reveals that he achieved descendancy by the size of his body no less than his soul. How else, in such cramped quarters, with the oxygen supply so scarce? He states that he anticipates an earthquaking struggle for uncontrol, to be known as titanomachy ii, soon after the rest of us arrive down there. He hints that he, cliff, will be pushed upstairs, and prophesies that as our population increases in number, as we're taxed more and more for the air we breathe, our holy partners will be progressively smaller and smaller until eventually we shall have none at all. Take cheer—he says we shall have no further need for such, by then we'll *all* be holy. Ionia, I wish you wouldn't stand up so straight, but that's neither here nor there." Saint Jones turned away, tossing his head and murmuring a few words of praise to our partner who art in ground, led them from the temple to the heaped shoes and socks beside the door. Shod he led them home again, in silence past the silent underearthly scenes which they all gazed upon with rapt downcast eyes. But once inside, in the corridor, he paused and turned to smile at Claude, placed a hand on Claude's free arm. "You like it down here, don't you, partner," he murmured affectionately.

"Yes . . ."

Saint Jones gave Claude's bicep a gentle squeeze. "You could stay, you know," he murmured. "You've got the build for it. You could bunk with Ionia." They were outside her cubbyhole. "No no, Ionia has lots of room. In fact it's our practice to get as many partners as possible on a single girl, it saves us space and serves as a stopgap method of birth control. In time, if all goes well, every girl will have her own diaphram —but I'm afraid that will have to wait on cliff," he said. "Well, partner? What do you say, are you ready to give up the sun and the moon and the bowling ball?"

Under the blazing lights, Claude and Ionia studied one another carefully aslant. Beneath arched brows her lustrous eyes reflected unspeakable daylight images, a nymphomaniacal mirage, in duplicate. She did not blush, far less perspire. "Saint Jones," he said at last, "Ionia. Thank you both for honoring me. I say to you in all humility that I don't think I'm ready yet."

"Partner, you're absolutely right!" Saint Jones agreed enthusiastically and patted him. "You still have work to do topside. Will you pardon us? We were merely placing temptation in your way, testing you. Truly the Choctaw have found their man at last! Partner, will you lead the way?''

"All right, Saint Jones." Claude did not only imagine a pale flush of biased hurt as he turned to lead the way back through the corridor, through the still astounding livingroom, through the opposite corridor, up those hundred steps with slippery leather soles trodding as lightly as possible on Ionia, hearing too the fearful mashing of Latvia, once removed, and finally letting loose of his scallion to press on before anxious apostolic warnings from below, "Hold on, partner! Are you still there?''

"Just fine, Saint Jones."

He held the trap door for them while they climbed out, Ionia and Latvia bearing corn, Ionia with a sullen groundling stare, Latvia sucking blood from her outside fingertips, Saint Jones puffing a little, shaking his beard, smiling his admiration for Claude and the Choctaw too.

"Lunch will be ready in a few minutes, boys!"

"All right, Saint Jones."

Outside, Ionia no longer walked with Claude but ran instead at Saint Jones's side and stared, obliquely, past the saint at Claude. There was little Claude could do to avoid her eyes, or avoid her significant nod at a power pole where perched a young man in oilskin slicker and broad-brimmed hat, high boots and gloves, scanning the highway through binoculars. "Oh Willie, I have your bubblegum!"

"Not now, Ionia," Saint Jones panted, but Willie blew a little pink kiss to her. At the van Saint Jones paused long enough to press Claude's hands in his, promise him, "Partner, we shall meet again."

"All right, Saint Jones."

"Dad, when?"

"Ionia, I don't know that yet," he said. "All things wait on the coming of cliff."

"When, Dad?"

"Ionia and Latvia . . . " he said. "Partner, what was that?"

That? That was the trunk, not just thumping now but thundering, and heaving on its springs. Claude grasped the handle, rattling it. "Not yet, not yet!" he hissed, "too soon, too soon!" To no avail—the entire beast rocked.

"Partner, you hear it too?"

"Yes, Saint Jones," he said, unlocking, lifting as slowly as he could. He held the trunk lid while Pete climbed out, while Pete stooped to dust his puttees off, adjust his gun, his badge, his cap, and then stood up. From the van steps Saint Jones too saw all this.

"Partner, where's he from?"

"He's just a friend of mine, Saint Jones, he just came in from Mexico. . . . "

Saint Jones's moon-size eyes measured Pete from top to bottom, side to side, front to back, and back again, before they sank out of sight. But when he spoke to Claude his voice was soft: "Partner," he said, with love, "you'll want to watch your load. That left rear tire is low." Now he ducked into the van, spread the van doors narrowly for his girls, slammed sharply on a last sideswept grimace by Ionia. Above the quivering doors sounded the counter's ungoverned clack, like blasphemy.

"Hey, who was he?"

"Partner," watching him, "that was Saint Jones," Claude said.

Pete rolled into the trunk, folding his legs the other way this time, laughing, remarking, "I didn't think he was the patrol, did you?" as Claude locked up. Left with his thoughts again, alone in the strontium, Claude backed the beast around, headed her slowly down the scratchy drive to the stony road, out onto the highway and on around that gently biased curve, which she had the modesty to hide behind before she shat a tire.

"Same one again?"

"Same one."

"She was trying to tell you for twenty miles, but you couldn't hear her with your radios."

"Couldn't I?" Claude held the trunk door up a few inches while Pete passed out the jack, the wrench, the spare, tossed out his cigarette too before Claude locked him up again. It took only seconds to rip off her skirt, prop the jack beneath her ruptured butt, decap, but those eager highwaymen had screwed on her nuts for evermore. He was sweating over the third one when a car approached, slowed down, stopped, in back, with blinking lights. This was one Claude hadn't seen before, and blue.

"Having a little trouble here?"

"Just this tire."

"Boy, she really exploded, didn't she!"

"I'll say she did."

"I noticed your Okl'oma stickers. I could spot them a mile away."

"You could?"

"Okl'oma City, eh? That's my town too."

"Ya, I'm delivering this beast to a lady there."

"Good old Okl'oma City. Boy, I wish I was there right now."

"Boy, so do I."

"Here, let me give you a hand with that. . . ."

"That's O.K."

"Here. . . ."

It takes two hundred pounds to fill the uniform. They were quickly done.

"I'll take that," Claude said. "I'll just toss it in the back."

"You don't want it mucking your upholstery up. I'll . . ."

"No, here. . ."

"What's the trouble here—ho, you must have had it lock . . ."

"Here!"

"Hold it—what are you doing in there?"

"I don't know." Pete already had his paper out, handed it out ahead of him. The officer glanced fleetingly at the paper, at Pete, at Claude. Then he fitted his bracelets on Pete's ready wrists and followed Pete to the patrol car, where there was some laconic dialogue on radio. Soon he sauntered back, took the shattered tire from Claude, tossed it in the trunk.

"I'm going to give you a break, Okl'oma," he said, dusting off his hands. "I guess you don't know much about our laws down here. My advice to you is, as soon as you get that wheel back on you hurry right on home. . . . " Pete was already in the car. The officer climbed heavily in with him, turned around, and headed slowly, it seemed sadly, back to Mexico.

Nor was it happy driving north, without anyone to understand the radios, without a secret ballast to calm the nervous beast, without a friend. Not even a thought in an aching head. Pushing hard, Claude reached Tucson a few minutes before his bank shut up. He chose a different teller this time, a bald, harried one, to ask, "Can you find out for me if my money has been transferred from Los Angeles yet?"

"Who are you?"

"Claude Squires."

The teller was gone a while.

"How do you spell your name?"

Claude spelled it out and the teller went away again. He soon was back with furrowed, wagging brow. "Did you fill out form 32?"

"Thirtytwo?" Claude filled it out under the teller's anxious gaze, slipped it under his splayed fingertips. "Can you tell me how long this usually takes?"

"That depends."

Thanking him Claude left for Mexico, stopping long enough at the hors d'oeuvres table to pick up a check.

The chief was waiting up for him, fingering papers at his desk, drinking coffee to stay awake. Both cops were there, enchaired. Both stood up, but not the chief. In fact he seemed not to know that Claude had arrived, so busy was he with his paperwork. But he noticed when he reached for his coffee cup. "Ah. Ah." He smiled, but there was a hint of annoyance about his eyes, as though he had witnessed a little grace in a stumblebum. "Sir," he said, looking at a paper on his desk, "what do you want us to do for you? We let you have this man this morning and they bring him back to us the very day. We know this man is always chronic, sir, but we never saw him come back so soon before. The United States Government is very angry about this this time. They thought we would hold him here a while. This time I have to promise them they won't have to worry again for thirty days. I don't know what to do with this man. This man deserves life imprisonment."

"How much will it cost to get him out?"

"This man deserves life imprisonment," the chief said. His cup was empty, he set it to one side. "I'm going to fine this man one hundred dollars," he said, "for offending twice."

"United States?"

"Always United States."

"I'll have to give you a check this time."

"Anything," the chief assured.

Claude took the pen he offered him and wrote out his check, postdating it a week. "I made it out for my entire balance," he said, while the chief studied it. "You can put the extra thirteen dollars on his account."

"Ah. Ah," the chief said, nodding, smiling, folding the check. He spoke to the cops, filled out Pete's paper while they were gone. Pete nodded to Claude when he came in, accepted his paper from the chief on his way to the second desk. The cops helped one another issue him his things. This time Pete did not take the time to put them on, but gathered them all together in one big hand, rather apologetically. Now they all walked to the door in a group. The chief, adjusting his hat, stepped outside with Claude and Pete, peered up and down the darkening street. "My car is in the garage having repairs," he said, shaking hands with Claude. Nodding amicably at both of them, he hurried home on foot.

"You got me out again," Pete said, shaking hands. "Now I owe you twice."

"This one's on me—you didn't ask to get out so much."

"You had to pay again, didn't you?"

Claude nodded, heading south. "Say, did they ever get a chance to throw those flowers at you?"

"Not this year," Pete said. "But that's all right, I have made my vow again for next year. Where can I send my hundred dollars to?" He held out his paper to Claude. "Write here," he said.

"Pete, one more thing. Do you remember Saint Jones?"

"Who? Write here," Pete said.

"I have nothing to write with."

Pete handed him his sheriff's badge, and Claude stopped the car to scratch his name, Claudine's address.

"Hey, did you see your girl?"

"Yes, I saw her," Claude said, handing him the paper. "Do you still want to go to Watsonville?"

"I don't care," Pete said as he studied Claude's writing in the passing car lights. "I don't think I want to try this time, do you? I think I want to go home and live in the past a little. You too?"

"Yes," Claude said. He offered to take Pete home, but Pete would not allow it for fear that he would never find his way back again. Claude didn't much care, and said so, and stopped the car when Pete told him to. It was dark now, a few car lights pointed out the straight black road ahead, and pushed the moonlight far out on the desert to either side, where it lay almost white. Pete put on his hat before he got out. He reached his hand back in the window, and they shook.

"Well, Pete, next time we'll find that treasure."

"Hey, sure we can," Pete said, shaking hands again. "Take it easy, hombre."

"O.K., Pedro." Waving, Claude turned the beast around.

"Goodbye, amigo," Pete called.

"See you, partner." He looked back, waving, but his sharp turn had left darkness everywhere but straight ahead. He drove there slowly, looking at each car he passed, wondering which one would stop to pick the king of the Yaquis up. Any Choctaw would, but do they often travel to Mexico?

Four

Before crossing the border he stopped for all the gas and oil the beast would have, the latest map of U.S.A. After that it did not take him long to count his change, or long to find that no route yet hacked would take him to Oklahoma City on twice this much, so he had to remove his caps at last and the attendant cheerfully gave him some of his money back, a dollar apiece, United States. Now with luck he might get as far as the Oklahoma line, perhaps the rest of the way would be downhill. If not, there was always Neely Air Force Base, or used to be. He knew where else he could obtain a loan, of course, but by the time he reached the Tucson limits he had dismissed this thought, he could not afford to stop, use gas to start again, and he could not reason with the motor going. Thus he glided stoically past MRS WHITES enticing blink, straight through the sleepy town, the six black neighborhoods, took off for the Pimpled Hills in overdrive.

He stopped once at dawn, for jam, on a steep downgrade that offered the beast a flying start, but decided to save the jam for lunch. Now that it was turning light he probably did not need the pabulum of the radios to keep awake, and yet he left them on because it pleased him to make use of his last resource, be a lavish wastrel of battery. A light rain blurred the day, showing him only a small part of the road ahead, lopping it off and narrowing it, treadmillwise, so that he had no sense at all of progress unless a gas station floated by, or he read his gauge. During the morning he stopped twice for gas, the second time saving his last dime aside for use in an emergency. He did not allow himself to check her tires. At noon he tuned in the Texas news, having memorized the New Mexico. The rain which had come as a gentle surprise to New Mexico was already flooding parts of the Lonesome State. Nevertheless Texas farmers were getting better prices than their neighbors for beef today, about the same for hogs, and lambs. Mrs. Clara Larson of Amarillo broke her arm last night on her way home from church, New Mexico hadn't heard that yet, nor that Ronnie Crittenton had won the Kiwanis what-America-means-to-me first prize. In spite of such enchantments, the gauge read worse than empty when they splashed over the Oklahoma line. Neely lay thirty miles, three gallons, straight ahead: he knew a few people there who might lend him gas if he got that far.

They floated in, without radio, the beast releasing her bated breath in silent little puffs of steam. Deciding not to waste his dime, Claude drove to 211 Elm. The rain had withdrawn into sodden quietness, and walking up the path he saw that they had lost one of their twin elms since he was there. Waiting at the door he looked at the sawed-off stump: its smooth top appeared already grey with age though wet. Inside, a flurry of footsteps hurried him back to an afternoon six or seven years ago, when the sun was out. He had been invited for dinner then, and for several Sundays after that, however many it had taken Neely to make a gunner of him. That first day it had been Mrs. Hoyt who came to the door, opened it just wide enough to look out at him, query "Yes?" with eyebrows raised, as she did now.

This time he had no olive-drab pussycap to doff to her, but he smiled as he had before. "Hello, Mrs. Hoyt."

"Hello, how are you."

"Just fine. How's everyone?"

"We're just fine." She opened the door wider now, if not quite wide enough for him, and there was a low cough inside.

"Is Karen in?" he asked, but did not need her surprise

to tell him no, for already he had seen the picture on the table in back of her, beside the tasseled lamp, and this was not the portrait of Karen decolleté which he recalled. This was a group portrait, the bald grinning man posed behind Karen with one big soft hand planted on each tailored shoulder of her green suit, the two babies on her knees looming pink and formidable, one almost a child. Claude looked away from them to a slanting mirrored portrait of himself, above, a scurrilous beard, an hair-streaked skull, a limp shirt on which Arizona dust had run to mud. "I'm Claude Squires," he said to Mrs. Hoyt. "I used to visit Karen when I was in gunnery school, about seven years ago. I'm just passing through."

"Oh yes of course," said Mrs. Holt. "I knew I remembered you. It's just that we used to see so many boys, we—I didn't recognize you without your uniform. . . ." Youth is a uniform. "Would you like to come in and visit a while?"

"I'm sorry, I'm just passing through. I have to deliver this car," he said. "I thought I'd stop by and see if by any chance Karen was here."

"Well, no, she got married some time ago. She married Coy Goff. Did you know Coy?"

"He must have been after my time."

"She married Coy about six years ago. Good gracious, it must be almost seven! Pappy—when was it Karen married Coy?" There was a grunt from the diningroom, at which she raised her eyebrows humorously. "Yes, it will be seven years in August," she said loudly, to both of them.

"Well, say hello to her for me when you see her," Claude said, from the path. "Tell her Claude sent his best."

"Claude—I know, you're the crewcut one!"

"That's the one," Claude said.

"Well. I wish you could have stayed!"

"So do I," he said, and waved.

The beast started, and took him all the way back to town, where he stopped before a service station, as close to the pumps as he could park her publicly. The smiling attendant glanced from beast to beard to bag before granting Claude the key, a new one chained to a two-by-four. The restroom was not so new, but he had had much practice shaving in the military way with right hand touching nothing at all save face, left hand doing the dirty work, breathing slowed almost to the blackout point. Once outside, he stopped ten feet from the door, gratefully gasping pure evening air and cleansing rain. Now it was the attendant who stopped in his tracks, with right hand outstretched; he wouldn't have smiled so efficiently if Claude had tossed his key to him. Claude hung it up. Not until then, on his way out, did he learn from the standard sign that his friendly host was Coy O. Goff, with cap.

Leaving the beast to bask in Coy's overflowing light, he headed downstreet into a familiar dark, past the sinister little bar where he had tried many times to grow befuddled on 3.2, past the rainbound movie house, drew up at the Friendly Cafe in a dead heat with the Okl'oma City bus. He stood aside while ten or twelve passengers filtered out and in, found himself a view hole in the foggy glass. He knew her at once by how she stood, the same aggressive stance, crosswise in the narrow slot behind the counter, her hip resting carelessly against the service table, her outslung bust in profile against the sandwich list, her cigarette balanced precariously on top of the coffee urn, her half-filled coffee cup beside her on the counter, close to hand, so that she could find it without interrupting her rapt appraisal of the inflowing customers. He waited, watching her look through three or four at a time to smile at one, until they were all inside, then he entered too. She smiled her quick, pleased smile at him, and then she remembered who he was. "Well now look, look who just blew in!" she cried, putting down her cup and facing straight. "I'll be damned. Gee, how are you, kid?"

"Hello, Fran," he said, sitting down before her. "Do you mean to say you remember Claude?"

"Why sure, like yesterday." Smiling at him, she almost made it so. Claude smiled too. She was about thirtythree now. Seven years in the Friendly Cafe had given her smile wrinkles a more various company, burned the dark coffee rings more indelibly around her eyes, left her glossy golden hair less wild. Seven years in the slot had left her with even less bodyroom than he recalled, but turning to draw his coffee she used it no less gracefully. "Did you come in on the bus?"

"No, I came by a less prolific beast."

She pushed him the sugar. "Well, hang around." He watched her move down the slot, choosing customers in her erratic efficient way, humoring some, ignoring some, as she always had. On her way back to the coffee urn she slipped a bowl of oyster stew in front of him. By the time he had finished that there was a thick raw steak, warm rolls, an outsized glass of milk. He was the first one done, so he went to the nickelodeon, gave up his dime for "Hard Time Blues."

"Pie?"

"No, but have you an extra cigarette?"

She tossed him her pack. "We can take off as soon as the bus leaves," she said. "I've been looking for something to celebrate."

She had the counter cleared and wiped before the driver got his motor going. Another girl was cleaning the tables, and Fran spoke to her before she went into the kitchen for her coat. Claude gave her back her cigarettes as they walked out.

"Where's your car?"

"That's it in front of Coy Goff's," he said.

"Is there gas in it?"

"Not much."

"Leave it there," she said. "I like to walk."

She took his arm and they hurried quietly, with lowered heads, through the steady rain. Her room was three blocks away, the same glass-porch room, its private entrance adjoining the unshaded parlor where the same grey couple sat dozing beside the same huge radio. The hinges were still unoiled—their screech used to unsettle him. Inside, the big bed, bureau, easychair, the high old cardboard closet, the heavy crimson drapes covering the three glass walls, as before. "Hey, you've got a new refrigerator," he said.

"Oh, is that new?" She was taking off her coat. "Take off your shirt."

She hung it up for him. "You should have a coat," she said.

"I know."

"Take off your shoes."

Seated in the easychair he took them off. They no longer smelled so new, but old and dead; he kicked them under the chair. The room was warm, heat seemed to seep through the door connecting them to the room with the radio. Fran turned her radio on. She went to the refrigerator, brought out two of those green bottles with the crookedly slapped on labels that looked handmade, passed Claude his bottle from the bed. Coogan's Old Style. Sighing he lay back in the easychair, a little farther from her old-style smile, said, "I thought I might find you married, Fran."

"Ha." She tilted back to drink. "I've had about enough of that to hold me a while." It was what she had said seven years ago.

"Was it Tom?" he asked. "Tom Jones?"

"Tom Jones, yes. The beautiful bastard." She smiled at the green bottle in her hands. "Say, you've got a good memory! But do you know what, I don't like to talk about him as much as I used to. In fact the thought of him almost bores me now. I don't hardly ever think of him any more. What about you? Where did they send you after you left here?"

"All over the damn place," he said.

"Where?"

He started to say, but stopped and smiled. "I guess that bores me too."

"Do you still live in New York?"

"No, my mother's in Boston now, and my father's out in L.A. I followed him out there."

"What have you been doing?"

"I went back to school a while, then I had a few odd jobs. . . ."

"Do you ever fly?"

He shook his head. "Airplanes stink—three parts gasoline to two parts puke."

"Not gasoline, not any more."

"Something new?"

"Well, have you met any girls?"

"No. One," he said.

"That's a hell of a lot more than I can say myself," she said, going for beer. "It's not so much fun around here since the field changed over to jets. They don't seem to get any live ones out there any more. They spend all their time walking around town like little business men, buying things. Then when they stop by the café they pile their packages in little piles in front of them, like they're asking everyone not to come too close because they're fragile and valuable. Then they tell dirty jokes about airplanes—" ("Ten years from now Neely Field will be a sales lot and they'll all still be out there selling used jets to the mice," he tried to put in) "and swill the coke in their mouths like it was listerine. If one of them does make a pass at you it's like he wants something to write about in his next letter home, like to reassure the folks. Crap, a girl could have more fun with a warm beer bottle," she said, taking Claude's from him.

He took his cold one up. "You mean they've lost their

imagination—they've still got it between the legs but not in the head?"

"I mean that, sure, I guess. What good is one without the other? Like their new monkey suits, they make them all look the same inside, no matter whether fat or thin. Pretty soon you lose your own imagination too. That's no fun." She got up to change the station, but could find nothing she preferred. "I'm older, of course," she said.

"You're younger than all of them," he said, "and you've got beautiful legs."

"So did you."

For now, that ended it. When she had finished her beer, she took off her stockings and turned up the radio. He sat looking at her while he finished his own, watching her move about the little room, brush her hair, lie back on the bed, trying to find in himself the whole world's shame for such a terrible waste. But he knew that pity could not make much fun, or love, so he placed his empty bottle on top of the warped cardboard closet and hung his pants over the refrigerator before he went to bed. She received him so kindly, so softly, that he could almost forget what a great deal was expected of him, although not quite. After a little play he called in help, first a movie idol or two, until they gave out, then a full Pullman-load of old-style raw recruits, one from each state, and invited her to chaperone them to their embarkation point, New York. Tom Jones soon turned up as a stowaway, but Fran threw him off on her way back to inspect the horsecars. The boy scouts, called up from the caboose, made a surprise attack, but they weren't needed tonight. When she was met at the dock by the Okl'oma State basketball team, just returned from a long tour of the Hebrides, she seemed quite satisfied with her trip. Well that she was, for he had accompanied her as far as he could. She remembered to turn the radio off, but not the light.

A rap on the door woke them up. His eyes watched

her smooth on her stockings and clip them to her garter belt, hunt around the chair for her panties and bra, wash at the sink, button up her uniform, but not until she stepped into her shoes was he prepared to recognize her. He smiled, and she clomped to the bed. "I have to meet the six-thirty bus. Go back to sleep," she whispered, kissing his cheek.

His body was more than willing; it was some firmer, or softer, part of him that could not lie there watching her button her coat. "Wait for me," he called, staggering up. "I should be on my way to Oklahoma City anyhow."

She waited at the door while he dressed. Then she wrapped the flap of her coat around his back and they stepped into the drizzling darkness, he embracing her beneath the coat, sharing with her what remained of the warmth they had brought from bed. Against the cold morning it wasn't much, but they did not run, for as soon as they drew apart they would give up what little they had, perhaps for good. Still they arrived at the cafe ahead of the bus. Patting farewell they went inside, and Fran went to draw their coffee before she took off her coat. She saw him shiver as he picked up the cup. On her way to the kitchen she said, "Take your time, you have to wait for the gas station to open anyway."

When she came back she brought bacon and eggs, a donut for herself, but she only had time to drink her coffee before the bus pulled in. He ate without watching her work. She had left her cigarettes behind, and he swung on his stool to look out the window as he lit one up. It was almost light, almost as light as it would be today: across the way he could make out the weeping face of the movie house, could perhaps have read the damp bedizenments. He went to the window and looked down the street. Coy Goff's lights were on, and suddenly he wanted to be gone before the bus.

"How much will you need?"

He hadn't known she was back. Sitting down he said, "Five dollars should be more than enough."

She had refilled his cup, and he drank while she took two fives from the cash register, scribbled the amount on a piece of tape. "You might have a flat."

Thanking her, he put the crackling money in his pocket. "I'll be able to pay you back as soon as I get to Oklahoma City, I hope."

She shrugged. "You'll always know where to send it to."

He had started to get up, but he sat down again. "Fran, why don't you come along for the ride?"

"Okl'oma City!" Laughing she shook her head; he thought her tousled hair looked young and wild. "Thanks, I've been there, I don't like the place. Besides," she said, patting her cigarettes into his shirt pocket, "I get roadsick. How about more coffee before you go?"

"No. No, thanks."

"Take care of yourself!"

"I'll be seeing you," he said. He waved from the door. He waved again through the foggy window and Fran, drawing coffee one-handed, waved smiling back. Ducking his head he ran through the rain to the beast, and she started up.

"Fill her up for you this morning, sir?"

"Yes, and the oil."

"Yes, *sir*," Coy said.

By the time he had finished, Neely was coming awake. Some lights were coming on, some others going off, doors were being unlocked, and a few of the boys in their plastic-veiled monkey suits were roaming the streets, ready to shop. The bus was still there. Slowing in front of the Friendly Cafe, Claude could see Fran's golden head facing a line of customers over the cash register. He gave a call with the wolf whistle and saw her look up—when she laughed he left quick.

[168]

Low down in the corner, one hand loose on the wheel, he let the beast do the thinking. She knew the way; and she cared. He let himself be enthralled by the soft siren song she sang to the road, how cruelly she spat at the other cars on it. Sometimes he helped her to pass one, for the pleasure of hearing her spit. Sometimes he spat too. But at last he grew annoyed by her eagerness to be home; he was eager to be nowhere, so he stomped on the brake. Too late. Oklahoma City, afloat in the rain, had come out to meet them halfway. He wasn't grateful: he had wanted to stop somewhere in the country for jam. Almost he could wish them grounded by the side of the road, or stuck in the mud, waiting for the highwaymen to come to the rescue. As for the beast, she was loath to slow down even now, even in traffic. "Where the hell do you live then?" he asked cutting her motor; she did not answer.

There was a telephone number on the lease, so he called. The operator asked for a quarter.

"What? Where am I?"

"You're calling from Yukon."

He gave her the quarter.

"Yes?" The voice, caught by surprise, a surprise, was worth paying extra to hear. She sang it again, that beautiful word touched at the very end by a hint of a lisp, like a kiss: "Yes?"

"Mrs. Merritt?"

"Yes, it is."

"This is Claude Squires. I've brought your car from Los Angeles."

"Ah, you must mean Puss!" She had an ear-tickling laugh. "How is she?"

"She's fine. She seems eager to see you."

"Precious! Can you bring her right over? Where are you?"

"I'm not sure, but this call cost me a quarter."

Laughing, "You must be in Yukon! You'll have to

keep on through Bethany to reach Oklahoma City. Do you know our city at all?"

"I've passed through it, but not very well."

"Well, just pass through it again," she sang, "and look for our house on the hill. You'll see our name on our gate on the north side of the highway."

"What color is your house?"

"Oh dear," she said, sighing, "I guess you'd call it tit purple," and hung up.

Back in the beast he followed directions, two miles past the city came upon a gate with *Merritt-Merritt* wrought on it. A cloud hid her house, but slaloming among the royal-eggplant oilwells in her front yard he had no doubt of its color, nor was he surprised by its size when finally it protruded before him at the top of the hill. It was her coyotes that worried him, two great brown coyotes with magnificent teeth that dripped a sticky saliva when they snapped at his window. He parked close to the front door, sat waiting a minute before he stepped out. The coyotes paid no attention, for they were around back of the beast ecstatically sniffing and wagging. A blond butler stood at the door.

"Mrs. Merritt would like you to park it in the garage for her, please."

Now the coyotes started snapping again at first sound of her motor. He found the garage in the rear, apart from the house, attached to the stable. The beast had plenty of company. Choosing a wide stall at the end of a row, he checked the glove-and-goggle compartment while he waited. Along with the wooden spoons Vivien had left the stone knife and the arrow heads; he took these with him going back for his bag, but now the coyotes were up front licking her headlights. He took a last look at her, patted her gascap on his way by: almost twenty years since he had had this feeling, of leaving a home.

The butler seemed surprised to see Claude again. "Did you wish to see Mrs. Merritt?"

"Well, yes, if I may."

"She's in the den." He nudged open a door on his way past.

Leaving his suitcase in the foyer, Claude pushed on the door the butler had started for him, looked into the den. There was a fire at one side, near a little desk at which a woman sat with her back to the fire, using its light for her work. A broad-shouldered woman in red, she had short hair that hung straight from her head to her neck like a heavy black helmet, unstrapped at the chin. She did not look up from her writing, nor puse, when she asked, "Have you delivered the car?" in the deep thumping tone of an oil well.

Claude entered the den. "Yes, I parked her in the garage."

"That's all right." She glanced at him. "What kind of condition was it in?"

"Well, you might have the fuel mixture checked," he suggested. "She seems to use quite a lot of gas. . . ."

"I mean when you picked it up in Los Angeles."

"Not too bad—a little dry. I had her lubed before I left, and the oil changed. I have the ticket some . . ."

"That's all right," she interrupted him. "I just want to know that the car's all in one piece."

"Oh yes—except that I ran low on gas money halfway out here and I had to trade the caps in. . . ."

"That's all right." She waved it aside, and beneath her dark helmet her gross face seemed almost to be smiling. "Does that little whistle still work?"

"Yes, it does."

Now she finished writing, waited rather impatiently for him to step forward and take the check from her hand. "Thank you," Claude said. "Thank you very much," he said, having read it.

"That's all right," she said, and he decided to go. But he walked slowly, feeling for his wallet, not wanting to leave the room with her check still fluttering in his hand. He had almost reached the door when she sang to him, "Would you like me to run you into town?"

Turning to look for her, he saw Mrs. Merritt look too, toward a divan facing the wall, where now a slender white hand slid over the back and up popped a head, a fuzzy rèd head with ears as round and big as its pale horn-rimmed glasses, above a loose, pink-gummed grin. "I'll be happy to run you," it sang.

"You won't run your car out of the garage again, Rudy," Mrs. Merritt growled softly, "until your sixteenth birthday."

Hurrying into the foyer Claude waved to them both and scooped up his bag. "That's all right," he called going out the front door.

A cloud still hung over the hill, although here in its midst it seemed only a fog. The coyotes hiked with him down to the gate, where they stood howling until he passed out of sight. In the city his first stop was at a second-hand clothier's, who dug up for him an old-style raincoat which could not be seen through, and cashed his check without questions. Outside he wandered a few blocks aimlessly, acclimating to his new confinement, before he entered a drugstore. After leisurely coffee he called the OK Drive-away Agency, asked the girl what she had going to Los Angeles.

"The nearest we have is to Phoenix."

"No, thanks," he said. He bought a pack of cigarettes and called her again. "What have you got to New York?"

"We have a nice little Ambler."

"I'll be right over."

The girl was just bringing his little grey car out from the back as he stepped onto the lot; she must have recognized him too, for she gave it the hotfoot, cut a tight turn, and skidded to a halt at his knees. Smiling giddily, she folded the babyseat and slipped it over the heaped boxes and blankets to the kleenex shelf, turned off the little radio and tossed him the key to his car. He listened politely to her description of its talents, for she had no way of knowing she spoke to a man on the rebound. He smiled when she mentioned economy. Following her into the shack, he signed the lease while she plotted his route to New York. His mission was to deliver the car, all the belongings therein, to the Kold Kash Kredit office on behalf of the former owners, who had got only this far in their quest for a freer life in the West. The girl told him all this sadly, for they had been a sweet couple, no ordinary jailbirds. She cheered up immediately at sight of Claude's fifty-dollar deposit, having no way of knowing this left him only forty. On the way out of town he stopped at a florist's for roses. "I'm going to New York," he wrote on the little envelope they gave him for Fran's money. "I wish you were coming with me as chaperone." But he didn't go back for her.

Now from his lowly, narrower view the day appeared to have changed, to have lifted, as he soon found it had. Out east of the city the cloud no longer sat on her hill, so that this time he could see her big house and, less clearly, her stable. The rain had stopped too. But the sun, when it shone, was behind him. Ahead, the clouds hung close together in groups, purple, swollen, uneasy, as though their bodies too were resistant to change. Lured by smooth roads onto a new turnpike, he read with surprise the rules he was handed, don't stop, don't turn around, pay when you get there; he made his escape at the first exit he saw, for fiftyfive cents, and now he was on the old road buzzing the staid turnpike by turns over and under, teasing it crazy. There was only one thing to mar his enjoyment: he noted that the turnpike was carefully bypassing a cruel-looking storm which the clouds had got up just to the north, while Claude on his road spent half his time prodding its edge, half his time fleeing it, lacing its bulges, in and out, like a little grey tip of a corset string. What made it worse, on the radio a voice regularly broke into the music with warnings, calmly listing most of the doomed towns Claude was dashing through. This angered him, for he did not like to think that he might die of penuriousness. He had much time to think about it, on this sidewinding road which he soon shared with no other cars, and yet when finally the city was in view he found himself still upright, so also the buildings.

They looked so familiar that for a moment Claude feared he had doubled back to Mrs. Merritt's city, until a sudden wave of water blinded his wipers and drove him along with everyone else to the curb, where the crackling radio reported an old man had just now been swept from his backyard by a cloudburst, the latest in a series deluging Tulsa. Clinging there to the side of the hill, no handbrake, Claude rode out the storm, stuffing blankets into the cracks under the doors, catching overhead drips as best he could with the babyseat. When the car next in front crept away from the curb, Claude followed as far as a gas station. There he wondered aloud what lay ahead, but the attendant couldn't say, having swum to work just five minutes ago. Now as Claude pulled away the rain suddenly ceased, it seemed from exhaustion, and for the next hundred miles he spun his dial to catch the latest reports: that old man was still missing, he had last been seen floating downhill toward the river, he had been found, he was dead, he was dying, he was still missing. . . . Claude turned off the radio, for he was beyond range of Tulsa, and Joplin had not heard the news yet. He raced in silence toward the night which he knew already had begun not far ahead.

Long before he got there the cooling air had sucked a thick fog from the saturated hills he wound through, forcing him to slow down and feel out the road writhing beneath him, his blinded headlights too straining to find darkness, something to look at. He was almost alone again, and lonely enough that whenever a car did approach he thought of his lowered headlights as more than a courtesy—a salute, sometimes acknowledged. He turned on his radio again, for a moment: one-year-old Billy Compton would die sometime after midnight in the gas chamber. . . . He turned on the heater. Even the hitchhikers had hidden themselves, except one six-year-old girl, wearing falsies, toting a big brown package on her back. He dared not stop. Yet he wished very much for a companion, anyone to fill the seat beside him as snugly as the backseat was filled with belongings, best of all that coyote at the racetrack in Sonora. There would be comfort in the warmth of his body, joy in the thump of his tail. There would be a reason for stopping every few hours, to let him run, to feed him canned manfood in the frying pan he had made Vivien. He had left that behind too.

With daylight (it was exactly a week since he last dressed for the office) he found himself passing through farmland over which a light snow had fallen ahead of him, softening, smoothing some of the rudeness, but not enough to hide the truth that nothing was planted. The day was cloudy, pale, as if out of kindness to the tall old houses that stood isolated from one another along the highway, behind their unshaven front yards, grey-and-white bearded, invariably two-storied, sway-backed, sunken-chested, dead but somehow still seeming powerful. Near each, a little behind, stood the dry shell of a barn, a neglected, overworked servant, ever faithful. Any one of these houses could probably be bought for a few dollars, furnished, there were probably even a few canned goods, perhaps a bottle of applejack not quite turned to vinegar, still in the cellar—a nice home for a month or two. Surviving farmers lived in new low white or brown houses, green-trimmed, with barns that looked like the schools of Los Angeles. He was in a way glad to leave Indiana, for there were fewer deserted farms in Ohio, and at Pittsburgh he took the new turnpike where there was nothing to tempt him but gas.

The time trials were over, it was time for the Derby. Challenged from behind by late starters, he took out after the pack, heard the roar of the crowd only a few seconds before all was lost in the whining and grinding of the cars he was passing. Now for a few miles he had the track to himself, only to come upon a new pack up ahead straining to escape him. The choice was between running them down or being run over: he chose wisely. Somehow, when he was not looking, a tit-purple sports-car driven by a big man with the silver hair and red nose of a champion sneaked by him; forgetting all else Claude concentrated on that driver's fluttering white scarf, until it passed from sight around the next turn. Left alone, suddenly more lonely than he had been even last night in the fog, Claude pressed on, the pedal now burning a deep hole in his heel, his eyes looking forward to nothing, for by now he knew by heart every foot of the track and the precise grade of each turn. And the signs: what to do, how to, where, where, until he had no ideas of his own. Except to refuel he stopped only once (motor running) at the midpoint, to dump his ashtray, topple weak and sway-headed back into the car. It cheered him after three hundred miles to see that sports-car again, easily catch it, incredulously pass it: the driver was sound asleep at his wheel. As soon as he heard Claude he woke and took off in red-nosed fury, and Claude, holding the Ambler to ninety, let him go. They met once again fifty miles later, but for Claude there was small comfort, this time he knew the champion had lapped him. He followed humbly over the finish line, grateful at least to have come in second.

Already the poor losers crushed unmercifully from behind, toward the river, all having heard that New York was filled to one short of capacity. Bearing down on his burning heel Claude submerged first. Still deaf from the race, half-blind in this unnatural light, it did almost seem to him that the beleaguered city had let water into the tunnel to halt them. But the indomitable invaders would not be denied, they broke into the city carrying Claude before them, north on the drive in a flanking maneuver, then east to engage the Fortysecond Armored Division head-on at midtown, mill there in the square in skillful confusion, neither giving nor gaining, deciding nothing, until finally Claude fled into a barbed-wire compound apart from the battlefield, an avowed coward, a prisoner. It took his last three dollars to bribe release for twelve hours.

Grounded, toting his dufflebag, he staggered through the streets with the foot troops, eccentrically yet not carelessly, to the Security Building where an old soldier still at his post recognized Claude at once as an enemy and delivered him without a word to the ninth floor. A man was locking up Kold Kash Kredit, but at sight of Claude he went back inside. A man made for smiling, he hovered near his desk, one hand at a drawer, waiting eagerly. "Yes, sir?"

"I'm delivering a car from OK Drive-away in Oklahoma City."

"Ah yes, the little Ambler." Relaxing, he played with his mail tray. "Where did you leave her?" He took the parking lot ticket from Claude's hand. "Have any trouble?"

"Not a bit."

"How do you like her?"

"Well, she got me here in thirty hours."

"You employed out there in Okla City?"

"No, I quit my job in L.A. . . . ."

"Hm. How you fixed for cash?"

"I could use some."

Shrugging the man put the ticket in his wallet. "It's my closing time," he said, examining his wallet. "Well, I'll give you your deposit, then we can settle up the oil and parking in the morning. If you decide you need a little extra. . . ."

"This is fine," Claude said, taking the deposit, "she didn't use any oil," and left quickly. Everyone else was locking and leaving, pressing into the elevators, pressing down, into the lobby and the street. Claude slipped out of the stream before it reached the door, stood pressed there with his back and his bag flat to a radiator, until he could get to the telephone. Virgil Cross, the one he wanted to call, would be leaving no office but would soon be descending from his room, his windowless studio adorned with black-and-white nightmares, to imbibe the dark hours with whoever happened along. It pleased Claude to remember the name of his landlady, Mrs. Lola Divers; but he did not find her name in the book. He dialed Information. She had no such listing, and he could not remember the number on Perry Street, if he had ever noticed. He sat on his bag, letting the book hang from its chain in front of him, for it had put on some fat. Reading, he began to understand why people like to tear it in two, there was nobody in it. None of his friends were—until finally, almost at the end, Timothy Zimmerman, who had taken the place of his parents. Big Tim was there and he would know where everyone else was. The polite lady who answered his telephone might have been Tim's mother, however odd that she referred to him as Mr. Zimmerman. Mr. Z was not home.

"This is an old friend of his, Claude Squires," Claude told her. "Is this Mrs. Zimmerman?"

"No, this is Mr. Zimmerman's housekeeper."

"Do you know where I could find him?"

"You might try his office," his housekeeper said, "although very probably he has left there." She gave him the number.

Tim was doing well with the ladies. This one announced Staken, Martin, Pool and Staken; the next, Mr. Zimmerman's office.

"Is Mr. Zimmerman there?"

"Mr. Zimmerman is just leaving his office."

"Can you catch him?"

"He's in quite a hurry. Who is calling?"

"Tell him it's Claude Squires."

"I'll tell him."

There was a wait and then a deep voice, but at some distance from the phone, sounding cautious: "Claude?"

"Hello there, Tim. Do you remember the voice?"

"I certainly do, Squire Claude," Tim said, much more heartily, "and the face that goes with it."

"I don't know that you'd recognize the face," Claude said, seeing it revolve nearby in the door. "How are you, Tim?"

"Still at it, and you? When the hell did you come back to us, and from where?"

"From the west. I got in today. Didn't I hear some little voices when I called your home?"

"Yes, three. How about you?"

"Not even a woman. But you were always ahead of me anyway."

"Yes—what is this, Claude, a migration or a visit?"

"More like a visit."

"Well damn. What has it been, eight years? I'm going out to Chicago tonight for a couple of days. I want to see you. Hell. Wait. Look, are you doing anything tonight?"

"No."

"Let's have dinner. I've got a date, but it's nothing important. My train leaves at eight-thirty. How about seven at the 42nd Street Longchamps?"

"Hell, Tim, I'd like to," Claude said, swinging the obese book on its chain. "The damn thing is I've got a few things that might take me a while. I'd hate to have you miss out on both your date and your train. . . ."

"Then how about a drink at the Biltmore at eight?"

"No, I'm afraid not that either. Look, maybe I'll still be here when you get back."

Tim's voice, when it came, seemed to come from that old cautious distance, or beyond. "Where are you staying, Claude, out at your mother's?"

"No, she's in Boston. Tim, have you seen any of the boys lately?"

"Hm, let's see," Tim said. "Not recently. I see Fred Reynolds quite often, he's downstairs with DeWitt and Blakey. You knew Fred, didn't you? He was two years ahead of us."

"Yes, I remember him. What about Virgil—is he still around?"

"Virgil Cross? The last I heard he was teaching in some little boys' school in New England."

"Teaching. I expected to find him still creeping around half-blind in his studio."

"Oh, that didn't last long. The army took him just a few months after he left school, soon after you left. I didn't like his stuff much anyway. Did you ever run into Bill Bollinger out on the Coast?"

"Bill Bollinger, is he out there?"

"He's in television. Bill and I were together for a while in the Navy. He and Georgia are divorced now. . . . Esther Newman is married—you won't have to hold her hand any more."

"How about George Moffat?"

"George and Alice are living in Chicago. I haven't seen them since they left, although I get out there quite often. . . . " George had been Tim's roommate. "You know how it is."

"Yes."

"I guess you knew that Milt Wise was killed."

"No."

"In a plane crash."

They tried a few more, all lost or, if Claude had not known them too well, successful or married. But, "Say, I heard about an old squiress of yours the other day," Tim remembered at last. "Diane Brand. She's at a place in the Village—the Top Hat Club or something like that. At least she was last week."

"Who's she singing with?"

"She's alone."

"What did you say the name of the place is?"

"The Top Hat, I think, maybe the Top Hole Club. Well look, Claude, I'm sorry we couldn't get together. . . ."

"I am too, Tim."

"If you decide to stay around for a while, give us a buzz—come out and meet the family. . . ."

"Thanks, I'd like to. It was good to hear your voice again, Tim."

"Yours too, Claude," Tim said heartily, from way out.

The lobby was empty and Claude left it so, cutting west before south, widely avoiding Big Central, to shave at Penn Station. Despite his precautions he hung up at each step, uneasily waiting to hear Tim's hearty voice hail him down, until he entered the white world of the shaveroom. He showered there too, and afterward put on his other white shirt, the one he had strained coffee water through coming back from Perhaps, but not up near the collar. Checking his laundry bag in a locker, he sat down for a shoeshine without remembering that he was down to his Kold Kash deposit. The man looked from the fifty dollar bill to Claude's shoes, to the two heaps of clay he had scraped from them onto the floor, and then he walked away. For quite a few minutes Claude feared that the bitter man had left him there forever, in business, but at last he returned with fortynine dollars. Skirting the ugly piles already being swept into a heap, Claude went to the bar. It took only an ounce of whiskey to send him reeling out the other side, dizzy with a vision of himself folding up there under the stools in the darkness. He stepped on his faraway feet through the station looking for somewhere he could eat sitting down, at last spotted a gap in the backs at a counter and steered himself to it, perched there between silent ladies who listened with him to his voice ordering coffee, milk, a hot roast beef sandwich. Waiting he sipped ice water, and wondered which way he would fall. When dinner arrived he was not hungry, but he washed down what beef he could, for the sake of the ladies.

That steadied him. Up on his feet, finding them as rocklike as ever beneath him, he plodded out of the station. Now the cold night air caught him up, making him lighter, just right for walking, and he headed briskly southward, out of habit, away from the majority. He was not wandering. Twenty blocks nearer the darkness he turned in at a cigar store, past the lonely man waiting among his keychains, to the barricaded hideout of the telephone. The yellow book flopped open to night clubs. It was the Topper Club, and it was not in the Village but on the grey lower edge of it. Stepping stiffly past the avaricious shopkeeper he turned to the south again. Down here he could walk more slowly, for although he was going some place it was not necessary to appear to be.

At night the Topper was alone on its dark street, on the far south corner, and it had to blink hard to let anyone know. There was no doorman, the padded door gave in easily, toward a reassuring darkness. The two men and one woman at the bar looked up from their stools at his entrance, for this was not a popular club and they were habitués. Two or three couples sat in the dark booths around the edges, a party of tired cats rested at a table in back, near the little stand where a fat man had for a moment played good lazy piano, but now a little too lazy, smiling to himself, as though it amused him not to do his best for such a house. It was the kind of place where Claude could have taken off his trenchcoat and still been served in unwashed pants and white-and-rust shirt. He sat at the end of the bar waiting and drinking fiftysix proof, like a misguided stranger. Two quick drinks later the piano player swung from his own bemusement into "Goody Goody for Me," almost crisply, and Claude swung around on his stool. For an instant, at sight of her hair, he went as silly as he had all through that summer nine years ago, when she had still been the first and he had still thought the only.

She wore it down to her elbows and loose, so that its blackness caped her white shoulders and drove attention to her white, white face with its bright slash of a mouth, its thin arching eyebrows, its sharp widow's peak which he knew to be carved out with a razor. She wore it no differently, the only difference was that now she was doing just that, wearing it, like a wig that did not belong to her. She was forty years old, and that many sick. She stood with both small hands clutching the microphone, swaying, sometimes with the piano, sometimes with her own music, humming softly, and staring out at the room with unblinking eyes. When at last, reluctantly, she took up the song it was no longer hers. Her voice at that height was thin and brittle, almost breaking, almost a quiet scream, as it had sometimes sounded to him even before, whenever she embarrassed him with a serenade while they were out drinking, with no band to control her. The microphone was frightful. But now she dropped into "Someday He'll Come Along," and that suited her better. It was almost as good as in the past.

The cats were getting quietly restless. The piano switched to "Take Me," and Diane gave up her microphone to move slowly around the room while she sang. Interpretive dancing was new to her act. She did it mostly with her shoulders, bringing them forward until they peeked out through her hair, while she sang to them, two knobby white islands about the size of her breasts, one at a time, then threw them suddenly back with her arms to cry "Take Me!" The piano player let a little mocking trill into each chorus, which the cats found impressive. One of them whistled. Diane said "Hi!" as she glided past them, and smiled at the ceiling. She danced among the tables, past the booths, singing softly to her shoulders, working her way around to the bar. There she stopped before Claude. He sat with his back to the bar watching, listening to the chorus, and then he said, "Hi, Diane." "Hi!" she said, gliding by. Back at the microphone she started "Baby, It's Cold Outside," and the cats stood up and filed quietly out of the room. Claude waited until she was through with her song.

He wandered, looking nowhere except now and then into dark window displays of books without titles, for comfort, or into whatever 40-watt hotels he happened to pass, wondering if he ought to spend part of his deposit on a room he probably would not sleep in. Finding no answer down here, he struck out to the north again. Soon he had caught up with the people, found them still away and racing in their four directions, still terribly concerned about something. Once he stopped in midstream to study them, to see whether they were miserable. He could not decide, nor could they, at such speed. Now he was going faster than any of them, coming upon them so fast from behind and head on that girls of all sizes and colors scurried into subways, men and boys would not look at him, but one undaunted old lady stood her ground and stared as though someone had unleashed a coyote in her city. He left New York at four minutes before midnight, by train to Greenwich, with the hope that there was still country out there.

The Boston Post Road had lost some of its glory since his day, but there were more trucks on it than before, and still room for pedestrians. The second truck, a big new one, picked Claude up. In the warm cab he dropped off to sleep almost at once, even though his interesting driver was an ex-prizefighter who had been forced into retirement at twentyfive by a head injury. They reached the outskirts of Boston before seven and Claude got out at a diner. He wasn't hungry, but it was a cold, early morning so he stayed in there eating until it began to look warmer, then walked quickly toward town until he came to a clothier's. There, for seven dollars, he found a beige gabardine suit, a bit wide-shouldered, that looked new except for one small frayed place on the back of the collar, as though it had been worn by a man who could move his head in a brace but was otherwise motionless. Had he died in it? If he had, why hadn't he taken it with him? It looked expensive. Claude sold his laundry and bag to the clothier for a dollar, keeping out the tie, the toothbrush, and the razor. He spent the dollar on a belt, a suede one.

Now it was warmer and he walked the five miles north at a leisurely pace, not to seem in a hurry and stir up the animals. Thus he reached the grounds rather late, at a quarter to ten. There was no elevator that he could find in this building, but he climbed to the third floor without being noticed. There was no answer to his knock on the door, so he pulled it toward him a little. She sat on the chair by the bed, with her back to the window, looking at a magazine. Either the sunlight that flooded her was brighter than it had been in her house ten years ago, or her fine blonde hair had turned white, even whiter than her cool handsome face that had finally begun to turn in upon itself, here and there, along conventional lines. Or perhaps it was simply her reading glasses that made her look like a mother. He stepped into the room, pulling the door closed after him, saying hello. She looked up without surprise to smile on him. "You got here fast," she said.

"Did you know I was coming, Mother?" he asked, kissing her cheek.

"I knew," she assured him. "Your father and Claudine knew too. We all knew."

"How?"

"Your father wrote me. I got his letter just Monday. By airplane," she said.

There was no other chair in the room. Rather than stand there hanging over her, he sat on the bed leaning back on his elbows and resting his right foot on his left knee in order not to soil the clean counterpane. Relaxed thus, he smiled. "How have you been, Mother?"

She closed her magazine, placing it on the dresser before she lifted her head to speak to him gently and sadly. "You're going to have to go back, you know."

"I am?"

She nodded. "Your father needs you. He has a job for you."

He placed both feet on the floor to sit forward. "Let's not talk about that now, Mother. How are you?"

"You don't understand, Claude," she chided him. "Your father wants to help you. He loves you."

"I know, Mother." He stood up. "What are you reading?"

Smiling, she shook her head sadly. "You don't understand," she said. "You just don't understand. Your father and I are going to remarry."

He stood at the dresser holding the house and garden magazine. "Mother, he's married."

"She has a weak heart," she told him. "She won't last long."

"That isn't the one!"

"The poor girl will be dead in six months," she told him. "Then your father will come for me in one of his automobiles."

He turned to look at her. "Did he say so?"

"He didn't have to," she said without blinking.

[186]

"That's why he went into his new business, his agency. So he might have a nice automobile to come for me with, so I might be comfortable when he carries me to our new home. That's why he wants you to go back to him, Claude, so that you may look after the agency while he comes for me." She smiled on him. "There now, don't you see how well things work out in the end? Haven't I always told you? Don't be despondent!" She patted the bed. "Come sit down by me, Claude."

For a moment he stayed where he was, because all at once this seemed the first reasonable request he had heard anyone make in ten years, and he wanted to hear it again. "Come sit down by me, Claude," she said, and reached out to touch his cheek when he had, saying, "Your collar is frayed."

"I know."

"Claude . . . " Now she took his hand and held it in her lap, stroking the bony knuckles lightly with her palm. "Please, please, let's not look so unhappy—for Mother's sake?" He managed a smile, she to answer it. "There now, isn't that better?"

"Yes," he said.

"There now." She gave up stroking to press his hand, tell him, "Poor Claude, you didn't have to come all this way to apologize."

"Mother?"

"I forgive you, Claude."

"Forgive me, Mother?"

Nodding forgiveness, "It was your fault, Claude. It was, you know."

"What was?"

"You couldn't know, of course, but it *was* your fault. Claude, it was."

"What, Mother, what was my fault?"

She was about to say, but she shook her head instead. "It's all over now, there's no use going over it again."

"Mother, going over what?"

"No, what's done is done," she said. She chafed his hand while it turned cold. "It's all over now. It doesn't matter."

"Mother, *what?*"

"Claude, don't look so unhappy!" she cried. "Please, please smile! You have such a *nice* smile, like I once did. Don't you remember how Mother used to smile?"

"*Mother* . . . "

"Claude, Claude . . . " She took his head in both her arms, pressed it hard against her breast, patted it.

"There there, it was just a little old tooth," he said.

"A tooth!"

Now she pushed him gently off, to cock her head and smile her scolding smile at him. "Don't you remember, Claude? Don't you remember when you cracked my tooth?"

He shook his head.

"You don't remember the broom?" she chided him.

"I remember your mentioning it."

"You were standing on the ironing board? I reached out my arms to you, so that you wouldn't fall, but you grabbed the broom instead? Claude, you don't remember? You don't remember cracking it?"

"How old was I, one?"

Smiling at that she shook her head. "No no, two," she said. "It was almost as though you understood, wasn't it, even then? My smile was always my best feature. Your father always used to remark on it." She showed it now, wide enough and turned aside for him to see the gap in it. "I had a lovely smile."

"You still do. . . . "

"It's ugly now."

"No, it . . . "

"Claude, Claude . . . " With a little laugh she gathered him in again, stroking his head. "Poor Claude, he never could lie to me. I could always read him like a book. Couldn't I?" Now she held him off to look at him. "Please, Claude, don't look like that! I forgive you! It's all over now, it's all right now, don't you see? We grow old, we learn, we learn!" she cried. "Claude, don't you *see*?" she cried as he stood up.

"Yes, Mother," he said, taking her hand from the arm of the chair, but she fell forward crying and it took both of his hands to lift her white head up from her knees. "Will you stop crying?"

"I'm sorry! I just hate to see you unhappy, Claude!"

"It's all right, Mother," he said, straightening her glasses. "Are you going to stop now?"

She nodded, and standing up he patted her shoulder, her back, doing what he could to console her. "Have you stopped now? Good." He smiled, for he too was crying. "I'll come back to see you soon. O.K.?"

She nodded again and he left. Outside the door he collided with a solid man in brown tweed, who cocked one heavy eyebrow at Claude's head. "Young man, you're in the ladies wing."

"I'm a visitor."

"Relative?"

"Her son."

The man took his arm firmly. "Mr. Squires, I'd like to talk to you about your mother's dentures. . . ."

"Her what!"

"They broke just last week. She's a lovely lady, I hate to see her smile marred so, don't you?"

"How long has she been wearing them?"

"Well, what, five, six years, wouldn't you guess? Of course, on her limited allowance we couldn't afford the finest . . ."

"Excuse me, doctor," Claude said, slipping free of the doctor's grip. But back in the room, where she looked up from her magazine with an unsurprised smile, he did not consult her. She had forgotten. Well that he returned though, for she remembered that she had some mail for him, forwarded by Claudine. The largest envelope contained a $100 money order, Mexican, with Pedro's "Hello Amigo!" on the back. There was a check from the office for the seven-plus days he had worked, accompanied by a note: "Dear Claude, Sorry to have missed you the other morning. Bronse wants to meet you when you get back—Yours, Franklin Storrs. P.S. We'll all go for a ride in my new English roadster." No word of little Ann. The last was a little blue letter, unperfumed. Redolent.

"Mother, I'll be back. Goodbye!" he said.